I0741634

Chapter 1

Sage pushed aside the tree branches. Piney needles pricked her fingers, the resin scent sharp in the thick forest. She gazed across the clearing to where Lakeluster House sat in the fading light, hunched like a troll near the small lake. "There's the house. It's creepier in the evening."

Her younger brother, Nate, pointed to the right. "That's where the body was found. In the tree."

Patrick thrust his chin over Nate's shoulder. "The victim was hanged, wasn't he? Next to where the swing is."

"He was, the poor man. One of my favorite teachers." Sage pushed down that upset and distracted herself by scrutinizing the three-story Victorian mansion, sagging on its foundation. One of the most vivid things about the house was the purplish-black paint on the old wooden exterior. "The place looks sad, lonely."

"And now people live there again?" Patrick squeezed between them. Since arriving to visit a week ago, their cousin had been begging them to come out here.

Secrets of Lakeluster House

Diane Scott Lewis with Jorja Parkinson

Print ISBNs
Amazon print 9780228635604
Ingram Spark 9780228635550
Barnes & Noble 9780228635611
BWL Print 9780228635628

Copyright 2025 by Diane Parkinson
Editor Renee Duke
Cover artist Michelle Lee

Dedication

*To my beloved husband George Parkinson,
who chose Nahant for the story setting.
May your journey to eternity be peaceful*

Acknowledgements

Thanks to the historical fiction on-line
critique group for all their help

"Ghosts or vampires should like this house." Nate shook his head. "The family left, years ago. They just vanished."

"But now an old woman moved in. With her butler, I think. She showed up six months ago, claiming she's the last of the family." Sage turned to Patrick. "Why did you want to come so late? It's almost dark." She tried not to sound uneasy as the shadows lengthened. At nearly fourteen, she was resolved to act fearless.

"We had to wait until dad snored in front of the TV. And mom left for her book club." Nate shrugged, but his face showed he too wished they hadn't come this close to dark.

"You say there's a butler? How bougie." Patrick chuckled. "But the house looks so spooky in the evening. That makes it more fun." He was close to fifteen and thought himself grown up—smarter than all of them.

"We've seen enough. Let's go home." Sage wasn't afraid, or so she told herself, but figured she needed to protect her brother who was two years younger. Even though he hated being protected.

"I haven't seen anything yet. I haven't been to visit since I was younger." Patrick tugged at the collar of his shirt, which displayed the name of his school: Hartford High.

"If your family hadn't moved away. Mom still complains that her sister's in Connecticut." Sage wouldn't mention the other reason. Her cousin had visited a few summers, but when his parents divorced three years ago, the visits stopped. Now he was here, older, and more curious about this dilapidated mansion in their confined peninsular community.

"The body was gross; did I tell you?" Nate's eyes sparked. "Skinned like a rabbit."

"How would you know?" Sage studied her brother. Such things usually frightened him. Though she knew he struggled to be tougher. "That has to be exaggerated."

"Kids at school said they saw it, hanged and skinned." Nate's mouth turned stubborn.

"I don't believe it, it's too revolting." Sage hid her disgust. She'd heard the same rumors. How could anyone have done that to Mr. Saunders? She cringed.

"I'd like to know more. I want to go inside to see what's left. Maybe something valuable," Patrick said in a tone he never used to have, something sinister, or cynical—was that the word? His parents' split had hardened him in some way. "There could be a skeleton or a treasure chest."

"I told you, there's people here now," Sage warned. Why did boys have few boundaries? Since becoming a teenager, having to deal with loud and gross teenage boys at school, she noticed this more and more. "We'd be arrested."

"We shouldn't stay long. Dad will wake up and wonder where we are." Nate touched his sister's arm.

Patrick stepped to the edge of the woods. "Wait. I still want to go closer."

Sage blew out an impatient breath and moved with him. "Not too close. We don't want the new people to hear us. And the house is so old, it might crumble down on you."

She glanced to the side, where the swing hung from a tree, outlined in the sun's last rays. The body was found hanging one branch over, the news people reported five months before. She shivered and rubbed her arms.

"We need to find out more about our great-great grandma who was supposed to have killed someone here over a hundred years ago," Patrick whispered. "That's why it's cursed."

A nightbird called from a tree, adding to the creepiness. An animal rustled in the bushes. Or Sage hoped it was only an animal.

"I've heard some of the story, but Grandma Jean said it was old folks' tales." Sage bristled. There had been whispers, odd looks between her parents whenever the manor was mentioned. She might discover more from her mother. It was bad enough they lived nine miles south of Salem, the town infamous for its witch trials. A sense of the otherworld always hung over the area. But she strained to bring them back to earth, to firm footing where she could balance. "There's no curse."

She glanced at Patrick. He'd grown taller, his bright blond hair turning a darker blond. He might be handsome if not for his crooked nose. Someone had hit him in school. If he kept egging them on, she might be tempted. Though her mom said she needed to start behaving like a young woman and not a child.

"Let's walk to the porch," Patrick urged. "Don't be sissies."

Sage swallowed another warning, but she had to prove she was as brave as he was. Still, he acted too ready to jump on anything and wasn't the kid he used to be. None of them were, really.

The three of them crept from the trees, across the clearing, until Nate hung back. "Do we have to go any farther?"

Patrick stepped beside him and pushed on his shoulder. "Don't be scared. Loser."

"Stop teasing him." Sage stiffened her back and walked to the three steps that led to the rickety front porch. A sudden breeze swept over the lake and tossed dried leaves across the wooden floorboards. They crackled like an old woman's laugh.

She tugged her sweater tighter. The weather remained chilly for June. The manor loomed above her, and seemed to lean to the left, its windows blank like dead eyes. Yet she had the sudden feeling that someone was watching them.

"Is this close enough for you?" She wrinkled her nose. The air smelled dank, almost rotten, then the breeze swept it away.

Patrick moved beside her. He hunched his shoulders, his grin not so smug. Nate hovered several feet back and kept glancing behind him.

The sun was setting, throwing deeper shadows over the ground. The two turrets with finials, and crooked chimney pots, made strange shapes. The place was built in the 1800s by a rich man named Brubaker who owned a fancy hotel for elite summer residents, Dad had told them. The rumor was that Brubaker wasn't kind to his employees or family. "Stingy" her mom said. And something shady concerning his first wife.

"We could knock and see if anyone answers." Patrick tapped the first step with his shoe.

"We need a good reason to be here." Sage tried to be sensible as her heart thumped. The house both pulled at her—a surprise— and repulsed her. "What *are* we doing, selling Girl Scout cookies?"

"That's funny." Nate made a nervous laugh, arms hugged close around him. All gangly at eleven, he seemed at a loss about what to do with his skinny arms and legs.

Sage wouldn't dare tell them that a few nights ago she'd had a dream about the manor. A dream with a strange little girl in it. A girl with tight, reddish braids, who wore a long dress and a soiled apron. She'd asked Sage to follow her. Then Sage had jerked awake, her mouth dry.

Standing this close to the manor porch, a chill crept up her spine. Her parents had always warned them not to wander out here, though they had when younger. "We should go, Patrick."

A window creaked open to the right of the porch. Sage held her breath. Nate whipped around and scurried back into the woods.

"The zombie is coming." Patrick snickered, his voice sounding more unsure. He thrust his hands in his pockets and peered toward the window. "I don't see anyone."

"A window can't open itself." Sage's words came out whispery. The window looked murky, almost swirly like the sea. She took a step back. Her curiosity was waning.

"Don't go yet. Don't you want to know about our great-great-grandma? My mom said she killed for love." Patrick's eyes glistened. "The answer could be inside."

Their grandma had never mentioned *her* grandmother and the ugly rumor, or changed the subject when Sage asked. But, yes, the whispers circled.

"It's too late now for that. I'm sadder about the death of my history teacher. Mr. Saunders was a nice man." Sage took more steps away from the manor. She'd enjoyed his history lessons, his pudgy, friendly face.

Why had he come out here? He often talked about the history of the Brubakers. Had he nosed about where he shouldn't? "The police don't know if it was murder or suicide." But skinned like a rabbit?

"We could find out more about the teacher, too," Patrick said, still staring at the manor. The window scraped open a little more. His chin jerked.

Were those fingers under the sash? No, it must be the damaged wood. Yet it had opened...

"I'm going after my brother." Sage's skin prickled. She turned and rushed off, relieved to enter the shadowed safety of the woods. Some secrets might be best left undisturbed. But she would question her mom again about their notorious relative. "Hurry up. You don't want to be caught by a ghost, do you?"

* * *

Jacob:
Children are snooping outside. Two boys and a girl. Hopefully, they won't try to come inside. The house is derelict, neglected, though it can transform when it wishes. The last visitor stirred up the...well, I don't want to think about that.

Changes are coming, I can sense it. But will they bring the resolution that's needed?

I know I've been here too long. Still, some of us have dwelt here longer. Do I feel remorse for my behavior a hundred years ago? Perhaps I should. Did I deserve what happened to me? I think not, but I am hardly without fault.

Chapter 2

Sage's mom, Jenny Emery, chopped onions with a sharp knife on her cutting board. "I'm very disappointed with you, young lady, going out there, dragging your brother through the woods when it was practically night. What were you thinking?"

Sage leaned against the thick plaster wall of the kitchen, just out of the pungent fumes. "Nate begged to go, but you're right. I should have told him no." She rubbed her forehead. Those supposed fingers on the window sash continued to bother her. It had to be peeling paint. At least the strange little girl hadn't entered her dreams last night. "You didn't answer my question about my great-great-grandmother. I know she worked at the manor."

Her mom sighed and straightened her shoulders. "We don't usually speak about that. But, yes, my mother's grandmother, Grandma Esther, worked at Lakeluster House. She was the housekeeper."

"And then something terrible happened?" Sage hinted. "Something romantic at first?"

Mom used her knife to scrape the onion bits into a pile. "We don't know the full story. I think you're still too young for those details." Mom stared down at the onions in case one might sneak away. Her brunette hair, the same color as Sage's, brushed her shoulders. Her stocky build, large hazel eyes, and strong chin also reflected Sage's looks.

"I'll soon be fourteen, ready for high school." But everyone told her she acted older than her age—*some* of the time. Too much reading? Unfortunately, there was no high school on their peninsula that dangled like a Christmas ornament from the mainland into the Atlantic between Nahant Bay and Broad Sound. She would be bussed to Lynn, the first town at the end of their long isthmus.

"Your grandma, bless her soul, asked us to never speak of the incident. Some people hide behind silence; it's how they cope." Jenny blinked her eyes; because of sadness or onions, it was difficult to tell.

Sage often thought of her mom as "Jenny" because she'd always seemed so youthful, more like a sister when Sage was a child. Though, since the *incident*, she'd grown more serious.

Grandma Jean had recently died. Her mom really missed her mother. Sage's throat tightened. She had loved her kind, quiet grandma, a woman who never spoke of her past, as if she'd only existed to be their grandmother. Grandma Jean had left the house a little empty without her calming presence, the clicking of her knitting needles always in the background. Was *her* grandma really a killer?

"Maybe it's time we talked about these things." Sage cocked her head with a small smile. Grownups needed to be coaxed in certain situations. Though Sage, caught on the verge of being grownup, struggled with her own tumbling thoughts. Her body was changing with more curves, and the doubts over forever leaving childhood clung to her. Was she as pretty and sturdy as her mom? Did it matter?

And what about her mom's silence about what happened two years ago? When would they discuss that? Sage pushed away from the wall.

Jenny eyed her, obviously aware of her game. She tossed the onions into a pan of sizzling butter on the stove. A huge hearth gaped beside the stove, a remnant of when their house was built in the eighteenth century. A cottage that had its own mysterious past.

"Where did Grandma Esther go after the...murder?" Sage asked.

"To the mainland to find work. She returned here with a new husband after her daughter went to college." Jenny tapped the knife blade on the cutting board. "Her husband retired to fish these waters."

"And Great-Grandma Barbara came back, too? Later."

"Yes. To manage the Tourist Bureau. She loved Nahant. She married a man in real estate, my jovial grandpa, and had her children here, including your Grandma Jean."

Sage bit down on her lip. She'd heard snippets of this throughout her life. "But no one proved the mur—"

"Please ask me more later. I'll bake a welcome cake for the newcomers. I heard the woman who now lives there is named Miss Dora Brubaker. You and the boys can carry the dessert out there tomorrow." She leveled the knife, her plump mouth pursed. "*In* the broad daylight. And be respectful."

* * *

In the bright light of day, after they'd traversed the woods, stepping over tree roots, the manor looked more dilapidated but less scary. Sage carried the Boston Cream Pie her mom had made to welcome Miss Brubaker to Nahant, the plastic serving dish cool in her hands.

"Why a Boston dessert when Nahant should have its own sweets?" Patrick asked as he kicked a pebble. "Don't we have a witch pie?"

"Boston's so close, we've been there many times. And this is my Dad's favorite, so Mom made two. Remember, be respectful." Sage had even worn a skirt instead of her usual ripped jeans. "And don't forget, you now prefer Connecticut."

Nahant had once seemed her entire world, but her world was on the verge of expanding, uncomfortable and exciting at the same time.

"Witch pie, that's a good joke." Nate didn't sound that amused, but he was eager to tag along. He stared over at the rope swing that creaked in a light breeze. Birds flapped over the surface of the lake as they crossed the clearing.

"Lakeluster? That's more a pond than a lake. A nasty, slimy pond," Patrick said with a dismissive air. Had the divorce made him so flippant, or was this his changing personality as he grew up? "And Connecticut's an awesome place." His statement came out irritated.

"I'm sure it is." Sage glanced at the pond. "I guess they use 'lake' since Pondluster House doesn't sound poetic." She hesitated near the manor's front steps. "Dad once said Mr. Brubaker had 'visions of grandeur.'"

Patrick mounted the steps and stood before the huge front door built in an arch. Purple paint had dulled with the years and was chipped and scraped here and there on once ornate panels, as though something feral had scratched at it.

Sage followed, her pulse tripping with each step. Her brother was close behind her. She breathed deeply; she must be brave, and she was curious about this place. She tried not to chew the inside of her cheek, an annoying habit.

Did their great-great-grandmother really murder for love in this house? Was that thrilling or just embarrassing? Or, most likely, a myth?

"Well, knock. My hands are full." She poked her cousin with her elbow.

Patrick gave a swift knock. They waited. He knocked again, louder.

Finally, with a rattle of a lock and squeak of wood, the door slowly opened. Sage curled her toes in her boots.

A tall, broad-shouldered man filled the doorway. He scowled at them, his sharp blue eyes fierce. "What is your business?" he asked in a British accent.

Patrick, Mister Bold, must have gone tongue-tied, since he stayed silent.

"Sir, we're here to welcome Miss Dora Brubaker to our beautiful village." Sage grinned, maybe too wide. "And you, too, of course."

"We have cake." Nate, hovering at her shoulder, said the obvious.

The man straightened, one eyebrow raised. He looked in his forties, though something about him, the longer style of his hair, the close sideburns, made him appear much older—or from a different time. He wore a white shirt and a dark blue vest over a slight belly, but no jacket. Butler-casual.

"Who are you three trespassers, might I ask?"

Patrick cleared his throat, finally joining in. "We're the welcoming committee."

"My name is Sage Emery. This is my brother, Nate, and my cousin, Patrick Clark." Sage's cheeks grew sore from grinning. This might be a huge mistake. She should never have allowed her cousin to nag them to first invade the manor.

"Who is it, Huntley?" a sprightly, almost brittle voice called from behind and to the right of the butler.

"Three children, Madam. With a cake." Huntley's voice dripped with boredom.

"Invite them in." The woman sounded nice, encouraging Sage.

He grimaced and stepped aside. "Won't you come in?"

Sage swallowed hard and stepped into a musty-smelling foyer, the dish gripped in her fingers. The room full of shadows, a stairway with a rounded banister rose with a curve directly in front of her. Garish wallpaper covered the walls, faded red birds and orange flowers.

Huntley watched them, lids half-closed, as if they were a science experiment. His light brown hair glistened under the high, rusted chandelier where five candles flickered.

Patrick moved in behind Sage. He glanced up at the chandelier. "Don't you have electricity?"

Sage glared at her cousin.

"Now there's a shocking idea." Huntley smirked and walked to an archway with scarred wood trim. "Follow, if you must."

Nate bumped against Sage and whispered, "I hope she doesn't look like a witch."

"Be quiet," she hissed.

"Miss Dora, may I present...three visitors with a welcome cake." Huntley waved a hand in their general direction.

Sage walked further in, the scent of mothballs strong. Should she curtsy, like in the movies?

The room looked shabby, the elegant furniture a dusty-rose, or just dusty, was worn. A short, round woman stood from a high-backed chair. Her eyes twinkled in her plump face, her smile sweet. Her gray hair was arranged in tight curls like a wreath around her head. Even her dress was gray, but shapeless, her shoes black and clunky, her stockings thick on thick legs. Even she smelled of mothballs as if she'd been packed away.

"How lovely to have three distinguished guests." She clasped her small hands together. The woman sounded friendly. She must have been well past sixty and her eyes seemed oddly out of focus. Poor eyesight?

"Miss Brubaker, my mother, Mrs. Emery, would like to welcome you to our village. She baked a Boston cream pie for you." Sage held out the dish, then introduced Nate and Patrick.

Huntley swept forward and took the dish. Sage felt odd with nothing in her hands as they hovered in the air. She clutched them at her sides.

Out of the corner of her eye, she swore she saw a mouse skitter along the baseboard.

"Very kind. You must thank your mother for me. Call me Miss Dora." Miss Dora beamed at her butler. "Huntley, do we have any tea?"

"No, please don't bother," Sage objected. "We aren't expected visitors."

"We just wanted to see the house." Patrick laughed, head cocked.

"Yes. True." Nate nodded, though he looked hesitant. "I like tea."

"Don't be pushy." Sage kept her voice even. "We wanted to be welcoming."

Boys! Sage would never understand them. What had her best friend Lilah said? That boys were only good to keep the population going? She must have gotten such info from her older sister. Why did her brother, once her playmate, at eleven seem more of a pest now? And Patrick was far worse.

A white marble fireplace on the right wall caught her notice. Carved ivy twisted up the sides, but why did it look as if they had tiny faces?

"You wish to see the house? Then you must have a tour. This home is full of oodles of history and some mystery." Miss Dora again turned to her butler. "Huntley, show our guests around the manor. I'll search for tea for when you're finished."

"It's hardly in a condition for visitors, Madam," Huntley said, his brow creased.

"Nonsense. Very well, only the next floor. Light a lantern. It can get gloomy up there." Miss Dora took the dish from her butler and nodded to Sage. "I must apologize; we're very primitive here."

Or they couldn't pay their electric bill? Sage dismissed that unkind thought. The wiring might need fixing.

Miss Dora gave her a sideways glance, as if she knew something about Sage that went deeper than this conversation. Sage's skin broke out in goose bumps.

After lighting a lantern, his disapproval obvious, Huntley returned to the foyer and indicated for them to walk up the stairs. Their feet brought squeaks and creaks along the treads. The deep shadows and dark wall panels here added to the feeling of entering a dungeon, high up instead of low. The windows to the left seemed to fight the light rather than let it in. The musty smell increased.

In a long hall with several closed doors, Huntley opened one. "In here is the private parlor. The one Miss Dora refurbished for her own use." He spoke in a distracted monotone.

The room was blue, a blue sofa, blue wallpaper, and a blue curtain at the window. The wood floor had a blue-flowered rug. A blue and white tea set sat on a low table. It looked unused, staged almost.

"What's on the next floor?" Patrick asked. "Is there an attic?"

"Dust and cobwebs," Huntley replied. "Not a place for overly curious children."

Then he lifted a high, smaller door on the opposite wall. "This is the dumbwaiter, which brought up food when the kitchen was still in the basement."

The boys peered inside.

"These other rooms are private or empty. The first Mr. Brubaker filled them with many guests when he held his stylish parties." Huntley opened another door. Inside the dim interior cobwebs hung everywhere. Dust and dirt piled in the corners. A chair was knocked over on the floor. No dust surrounded it, as if something bad or dangerous had recently happened. But the strangest thing was no one else seemed to notice, only her.

Huntley, expression blank, shut the door and walked back toward the stairs, the lantern light bobbing.

Patrick pushed on the wall panels. "Are there secret passages? Don't all old houses have secret passages?"

Nate covered his mouth as if fighting a laugh.

"Please try and behave," Sage said, but she too studied the panels.

The boys hesitated near the banister. "This tour sucks, bro. I want to see the attic," Patrick groaned.

"Maybe there's a skeleton up there." Nate stared at the ceiling, which had decorative plaster squares. "Or ghosts."

"Where's the stairs to the next floor?" Patrick asked.

Sage paused at the dumbwaiter. "We need to chill ourselves." She *was* turning into her mother. She was curious, too, more than she thought she'd be; but there must be a better way to explore.

"You never know, do you, about passages and attics? And things that go bump in the night." The butler glanced over at her, his eyes in wary slits. "Miss Emery, you and these young men need to come back downstairs with me."

Why, suddenly, did she feel this was all an act? A bad play at her school. Or he was hiding something and wanted them out as quickly as possible.

Sage started to follow but a movement in a corner startled her. She stared harder. An outline formed into a woman in a long apron, deep despair in her eyes, a pistol in trembling fingers. The figure opened her mouth, but no sound came out. Then she stepped back, flattened, and dissolved into the shadowed corner. A spike of cold chilled the air, then it too disappeared. The wall panel where the woman vanished seemed to move in and out, as though breathing.

Sage's heart in her throat, she gripped her hands together. Her entire body quaked. Had she imagined it?

Chapter 3

Patrick fired up the computer in Nate's slanted ceiling bedroom plastered with posters of anime characters. The Japanese cartoon people in flashy colors stared down with their huge eyes. Nate loved the action-packed cartoons with futuristic themes. Sage felt she was growing above such interests. She liked to create art with make-up, or other materials, someone's face a canvas.

"We might be able to find information on the murder on the internet." Patrick checked one search engine after another. "Can't find anything; stupid. I don't—"

"Let me do it. I'm good with computers." Nate slid his chair over and bumped Patrick to the side.

Sage watched anger darken Patrick's face. He'd certainly changed, once an active, laughing boy who ran rings around her. One who loved to play on the beach, always friendly. It added to her uneasiness after seeing, or *not* seeing, the woman at the manor earlier that afternoon. Her heart thumped as she tried to figure it out. She'd told no one. The boys might laugh at her 'vision'. Why was she the only one to see it?

And Patick. She'd heard her parents whisper about the divorce, his father deserting their aunt for another, younger, woman. Her cousin, an only child, must be devastated, but he'd said nothing. And she didn't know how to bring up the subject—though she understood the turmoil, or close to it, more than she liked to remember.

"Patrick, let Nate look." She smiled into his frown as she sat on Nate's messy bed. She was becoming quite the go-between. Was it a position she wanted?

Patrick and family had moved off Nahant when he was in fourth grade when his father changed jobs. But they'd visited each other, until his father decided to change women. Then their mom had frequently gone to Connecticut alone to console her sister.

"Sometimes you can find old newspaper articles about stuff." Nate's fingers tripped across the keys.

"Look at Boston or Salem," Patrick said, voice loud, as if he needed to hold tight to some control.

"Or a local paper, but they may have nothing online." Nate stared as words flashed on the screen. More clicks, hundreds of words, tons of scrolling.

"Wait." Sage pointed. "'Murder in paradise'. That could be it."

"This almost-an-island is paradise?" Patrick scoffed.

"It was picked up from the *Lynn Gazette* by the *Boston Tribune*." Nate clicked on the site. "This happened in the 1920s. Ancient."

"Scan the article, look for important words," Patrick urged. "Something gory."

"There it is, Lakeluster House, *the elegant home of the former hotel magnate, Harrison Brubaker*." Sage studied the screen.

"There's not much. A housekeeper was rumored to have killed another servant in the manor. But there wasn't enough evidence to charge anyone." Nate continued to scroll.

"They don't even name them. Then the housekeeper vanished?" Patrick thumped on the desk. "How could our great-great-grandmother just vanish?"

"She didn't. She left Nahant for another job," Sage said. "My mom said as much."

"How could she kill someone?" Nate's eyes flashed.

"It might have been a lover's quarrel, the paper hints." Sage peered closer. "I'll bet the Brubakers hid most of the details to avoid a scandal. Maybe she was innocent."

A grainy black-and-white photo showed the house, and an image of the original owner Harrison Brubaker—a man with a narrow face and solemn features. But no photo of the alleged killer, or who was killed, other than "another servant". Sage needed to find a picture of her Two-Greats Grandma Esther. Would she look like the ghostly woman? She tightened her fingers on her knees.

"Miss Dora said we could come back to visit." Patrick tapped his chin. "But how do we get past Huntley to the upper floors?"

Sage remembered trembling fingers holding a pistol. Had she really *seen* that? She blew out a slow breath. "Maybe we don't need to sneak around upstairs." What would they find?

"Do we really want to see a creepy attic?" Nate continued to check newspaper sites.

"You're both losers. This is an adventure, and our family history." Patrick stood, his hands fisted. "I want to explore that house."

Twenty minutes later, Sage found her mom on her own computer atop the tiny desk wedged in the low-beamed dining room corner. She checked and reviewed medical files and records for a hospital corporation and was lucky to work from home.

"Mom, do you have any photos of Great-Great Grandma Esther?" She tried to shuck off her irritation at Patrick for calling her a loser...and Nate, too.

The front door opened. Sage turned to see her father with his usual grin. The 'mask' she called it now. Tall, lean, with black hair, he was a handsome man. The old lady at the pharmacy said he resembled Gregory Peck, whoever that was. She had Googled him; not bad looking. Her dad worked as a science professor at Salem State University, a half hour away on the mainland.

Mom continued to concentrate on her screen. "I think I have pictures, Sage. I'll have to look in my albums."

Dad came over and pressed Mom's shoulder. A lot had cooled between them in the last two years, but it appeared to be warming again. Or so Sage hoped.

"Evening, dear." He kissed the top of Jenny's head.

"Evening, Ron. I'll start dinner in a moment." Mom's voice came out not-so-forced-bright.

He turned his smile on Sage. "And here's my smart daughter, about to start high school. Makes a guy proud."

"*Dad.* You're embarrassing me." Sage turned away, her cheeks hot. Why did she find his words not as sincere as they could be? Was she being fair?

Her father might have been following the terrible example of Patrick's dad. Yet her parents seemed to have worked it out, somewhat.

Sage swallowed past the lump in her throat. She wanted to trust him again. But she'd changed, too, after the 'wrenching incident'. "See you at dinner, Dad. Let me know what you find in your albums, Mom."

Sage wandered back upstairs to her bedroom. She picked up her phone and texted her BFF Lilah. *You'll never believe what we did today.*

* * *

Sage and Lilah Tuckerman left Cliff Street, passed the peaked, red-roofed village church, and stepped along the rocky coast. Various seabirds floated and cawed in the blue sky.

Sage had learned in school this land had been used for cattle grazing in colonial days, but then became a center for fishing and tourists. The tourists liked the beaches, sunbathing like greasy oysters on their towels, and boating in their fancy boats. That's why the hotels were built, and Harrison Brubaker, an outsider, made his money.

"I can't wait for high school to be over, and we haven't even started classes." Lilah laughed, holding her light jacket around her slender form, her long legs in purple leggings.

Sage envied her friend's model-like body. "We can go to college together, if we both get into the same one." Sage intended to be a famous make-up artist, and work on the stage, in movies or television.

"Leaving this place forever will be cool." Lilah twirled, her long, light-blonde hair blowing in the breeze. "Having four brothers and sisters is suffocating. They argue about everything while my mom yells at them.

Dad's always busy with his navy career. I need freedom, a city, like Boston, with culture. Or New York."

"Culture? Music, theater, places to dance." Sage smiled, picturing herself growing a little taller, looking fine in a sparkly dress. Or would she miss her island strung from the mainland on its sandy isthmus with the one road in? Would her parents' marriage survive when she and Nate moved away? Things were so much simpler when she was a little girl.

Lilah bumped her shoulder. "So, you told me about the manor house, but what have you found out about your, what was it, two greats of a grandma?"

"Yeah, Grandma Esther. We're still looking at news articles online. A servant, could be my relative, might have killed another servant. My cousin was really interested, but now I am, too." Could Sage tell her friend about the vision of a woman with a gun? "A love story, gossip has always said, but the papers gave few details."

"Or a *I hate you because you don't love me* story." Lilah put her hands on her hips. "What about our teacher? Why was he murdered? The cops know nothing, and now the house is occupied again."

Sage felt a chill that had nothing to do with the wind. "That's the saddest part. I never knew Grandma Esther, but I liked Mr. Saunders. I'm sure they're still investigating." She wouldn't mind doing a little investigating on her own, which surprised her, but where to start? "He always acted interested in the manor's history."

"Was he snooping where he shouldn't?" Lilah rolled her eyes dramatically. "But I liked him, too. He wasn't one of the, 'hurry up and finish and get out of my class', teachers."

From the cliff above Forty Steps beach, the waves of Nahant Bay crashed against the shore. Rocky outcroppings of crunched-together stone fingered into the bay. The small beach would soon be half swallowed by the tide.

At the top of the steps, Lilah threw up her arms "When I'm a legendary actress, you will do all my make-up, and we'll live in Greenwich Village among the artists."

"That sounds interesting. You won't need much make-up, unless you're playing a cat or something. But you'll have to pay me lots of money." Sage laughed and snapped her fingers.

They rushed down the steps as they always did since children, the stairs a twice switch-back down the cliffside. When they reached the bottom, their combat boots clumping on the wood, they were both laughing.

They'd run up and down these steps since able to walk, along with other friends. Sage had been a tomboy, climbing over rocks and ducking into caves, her knees bruised and scraped. A time when the ocean around them seemed endless, and their island was the center of her universe.

"Let's look for more sea glass," Sage said, catching her breath. "The old lady in town still likes to make jewelry from it."

"Okay. Hey, do you know?" Lilah swept her hair behind her shoulder. "My grandpa once said more than one person vanished from Lakeluster House."

"More mysteries. All the spooky tales we grew up with; ones my parents rarely spoke about in front of me. And my grandma refused to talk about it." Now that her Grandma Jean had passed, the desire for secrecy wouldn't matter if Sage poked around.

Sage stared off over the water, a huge wet expanse that had surrounded her, her whole life. Was it a protective force or a place of exile? "Lilah, do you believe in ghosts?"

"If I saw one I might." Lilah bent to search among pebbles. "Why?"

"I'll text you later. I have more stuff to look up." Maybe Patrick was right. They did need to get back into the manor. "For some reason, this is starting to fascinate me."

Chapter 4

Sage scrutinized the old picture Mom handed her at the kitchen table. It was difficult to tell if this woman, her Grandma Esther, was the vision who'd frightened her at Lakeluster House.

Her relation stood on a front porch, with a wary-looking girl with huge eyes beside her. The image was faded in the dull black-and-white format. Grandma Esther's hat obscured most of her hair and was pulled low on her forehead.

"Is this Great-Grandma Barbara with her?" Sage touched a finger to the girl, who appeared tired of standing for the picture. A tedious process before modern phones and digital cameras, her dad had told her. People had to stand still for long minutes while a bulky camera was prepared. Sage couldn't imagine a life without 'selfies' and instant posts to social media.

"Yes. I wish she hadn't died shortly before you were born. She was a kind, funny, ready for anything woman. Much more open than my mother." Mom folded towels on the table, next to the album from where she'd extracted the photo. There were others, but none this close up, as if Esther was camera-shy. "She also had two sons. One was killed in World War I."

"You promised to tell me about the myth of why the murder happened? And what happened to Grandma Esther after that?" Sage looked again at the photo. Now the woman's eyes seemed to stare right at her, filled with the same despair Sage had witnessed in the apparition at the manor. A plea for help, even. Sage shivered and dropped the photo near the album.

"It wasn't a myth, exactly. According to my Grandma Barbara, her mother worked as the housekeeper at Lakeluster House in the 1920s. Everything seemed fine, until there was a shooting, and a man was found dead." Mom looked down and slowly folded hand towels on top of the larger towels, the colors in pastel pink, brown, and lavender.

"This dead man worked at the manor, too, supposedly?" Sage picked up a washcloth and folded it, the soft cloth smelling of floral fabric softener.

"A valet of sorts to the then current scion of the Brubakers." Mom lifted her chin in a haughty expression. "Lawrence, I believe; he had a wild reputation."

"And the housekeeper was the reason for the valet's death?" Why wasn't her relative hauled off to prison?

"She was suspected, but it was never proven. An 'attachment' was alleged between Great-Grandma Esther and this valet, but anyone could have killed him." Mom stuffed towels into the plastic laundry basket. "It was a scandal the Brubakers tried to hush up."

"What happened to Grandma Esther after that, when she left here to work somewhere else?" Sage turned her back on the photo now lying on the table, begging her to look again. Her vision *had* been holding a pistol.

"According to my grandmother, she went to the mainland and found work as a woman in charge of a retirement home. Her first husband, our relative, died during the Spanish Flu epidemic after the first world war, that's when she became the housekeeper at the manor—a menial job, but she needed money. Women had few career choices then." Mom gave her a sad smile. "As you're aware, my mother didn't like to speak of the event."

That's how some people were, Sage had learned; ones who liked to blast their private business everywhere, and others who kept it hidden to prevent the truth from hurting them. Even her own mother kept secrets. "I wish I could find out more details."

Patrick ran through the kitchen with Nate chasing him. "You'll never catch me; I'm the fastest running back on my high school team."

"And I'm the smartest kid in my math class." Nate laughed, as if that absurd reply gave him speed.

"Boys. Take your game outside, please." Mom pointed at the kitchen door. They both, elbows poking, opened the door and ran into the yard.

"Were you ever curious about the manor's history?" Sage asked. Her mom's family had been on Nahant since it was first settled by colonists. Her dad's family came from Boston.

"Of course, but I hated to upset my mother. My grandmother and I had a few conversations. Like I said, your Great-Grandma Barbara returned to Nahant and married a local man. I'll tell you more another time."

Always another time. Sage walked away from the table. She had a sudden idea. What if the manor held information, like in books, photos, about its past? Would Miss Dora allow her to look? There had to be more to all of this. And she still fretted over who killed her teacher. Had he discovered an ugly truth?

* * *

Sage stood on the front porch of Lakeluster House. It was Saturday, and her father had taken Nate and Patrick fishing in a cove along their coast. The perfect opportunity to slip off to visit the manor, alone.

The door opened after her knock, and Huntley glared down at her. "Good day, Miss Emery. What is it you wish today?" He leaned against the doorframe, arms crossed, as if she was definitely an annoyance he didn't care to bother with.

"Is Miss Dora in?" Sage tried her brightest smile.

"She is resting, and not available for company." He straightened, as if remembering he should. His British accent intrigued her, even with the rejection.

"I wondered...if the house has any history written down. Such as books, an archive of some kind—"

"A library, do you mean?" He scanned his sharp blue eyes over her, his defined cheekbones etched sharper in his handsome face. Handsome for an older man, that is. But those eyes could shred you to ribbons.

"That's it, a library." She stiffened under his scrutiny. Would he chase her off? Would Patrick be angry that she came here alone? It seemed too many people interfered with what she wanted to do—now that she'd made up her mind to investigate.

"Why are you so interested in this house?" he asked, though his expression appeared to show that he already knew.

"My family, in the past, worked here." How much should she admit to? "I'd really like to know more."

Huntley arched a brow and opened the door wider. "I actually shouldn't. But I suppose I can show you the library, Miss Emery. Since it's just you, and not your boisterous entourage."

Surprised he didn't want to hear more, she followed him inside before he changed his mind. Maybe he didn't know about the murder. "Thank you."

Of course, without the boys, she felt more vulnerable.

Huntley walked to the left, the opposite of where they'd gone last time. They passed through a room with heavy, almost medieval furniture, and an Oriental rug at its center. Huge paintings hung on the wall. Fields, streams, and forests in muted colors. Was this once a dining room, but now had no table and chairs?

The butler opened a door in a dark-paneled wall and ushered her inside.

Sage entered and her breath caught. Floor to ceiling shelves lined two walls, all stuffed with books. Two large windows were on the left wall. A fireplace on the right-hand wall, with bookshelves surrounding it, had lions carved into its dark wooden surface. Their blank eyes stared out at the room. Three candles burned in a brass candelabra on the mantel, before a burnished mirror, as if her request had been expected.

She tightened her fingers. *Impossible.*

A desk with many drawers sat at the center, on another Oriental carpet. The scent of wood polish and burning wax gave the room a feeling of comfort. Something she hadn't felt in the rest of the house.

How could this room look so elegant, well-stocked and touched up, after the many years of abandonment? Surely Miss Dora hadn't brought all these books with her?

When Sage stepped farther in, to her right she noticed a gold-toned globe that sat on a cherry-wood stand, but the small table beside it stopped her cold. Iron handcuffs, an iron chain, and long dangerous-looking iron scissors were displayed.

"Is this the torture collection?" she asked to dispel her uneasiness.

Huntley smiled, slowly. "It's how we detain nosy guests and visitors, in the basement."

She forced a laugh, refusing to allow him to scare her. Was he teasing? "Can you show me where I might search for books on the house's history, any photographs?"

Her ghostly vision had made her more determined to find out the details. She'd never believed in ghosts before—before she'd seen one. *I'm sure I saw it!*

He walked over to the back wall and pulled two books and a photo album from a shelf. Again, as if anticipated.

She fought a shiver.

"You should start with these." He placed them on the desk. "Be gentle. They're old, and the old need caring for. I will leave you to it."

Huntley left and she let out a relieved breath. She didn't wish him hovering about while she searched. Although, he seemed a mystery to explore as well.

Sage flipped through the first book, releasing a mildewed smell. The history of the Brubakers from the 1700s on. Originally from England, migrating to New York, they delved into shipping in colonial times; then other types of transportation. Finally, Harrison started his hotel business, putting up rich tourists on Nahant in the 1860s.

Something creaked in the corner to the left of her. Sage stilled her breath but saw nothing, only shadows. A book was pulled partway out. Had it been like that before?

She returned to the history book.

Harrison's descendant, Lawrence Brubaker, was the owner in the 1920s. The last resident-owner, probably Miss Dora's grandfather, was Michael Brubaker. But Lawrence was the one Sage was interested in. He would have lived here when the murder took place, as her mom had said.

She searched the second book, which had more info on Lawrence, a man labeled a playboy, always sailing his yacht, surrounded by beautiful women. He also married a few times, though just when it was getting noteworthy, she turned the page and...something was missing. She turned back. Pressing the book flatter, she bit the inside of her cheek. A page was missing, carefully cut out.

"What are you looking for?"

A child's voice. Sage whirled around.

A little girl of about ten years old, in an old-fashioned gown and apron, stared up at her. She had a pale face, her reddish hair in tight braids. A white ribbon in a bow was pinned to the back of her head. Her large green eyes were shadowed.

"Hi, I'm Sage. I'm...doing research. What's your name?" She had no idea a child lived here.

"Bella Porter." The girl didn't smile, her gaze intense. "But anything could be a name."

A weird response. "Do you live here?" Sage felt the room go colder, as if someone had opened a window. She rubbed her arms. "Is Miss Dora your aunt or...?"

"My room is upstairs, on the third floor." Bella cocked her head. "I don't come down often."

She had a stilted cadence to her speech, as if she only recited lines written by somebody else. Or she'd repeated them many times before.

"Are you all right?" Sage wondered why she'd ask that. Was this child a prisoner, or a guest? Or just an odd family member? Then Sage remembered the dream she had of a child. A child who resembled *this* one. How could that be? Her heart twitched. "Do you... like it here?"

"Why wouldn't I?" Bella frowned. "It's my home now. But the others never liked visitors."

"The others?" Sage felt for a moment she was being pranked. She shook her head. "Um, okay. There's a photo album here. Would you like to look at the pictures with me?" Sage turned to the desk and opened the album, at first filled with sepia pictures with posing, glum people: fusty and dusty. Maybe she could get the child to tell her more. A chill crept up the back of her neck and she looked behind her.

Bella was gone.

Sage scanned the room, and it was empty. A lion carving in the fireplace mantel had its eye on her, a live eye that blinked! Sage gasped. The eye returned to plain wood. *Big yikes?* She stepped over and tentatively touched it, cool and wooden as could be. Then she looked down and cringed.

Bella's ribbon, still in a bow, lay on the fireplace grate.

Chapter 5

Sage swallowed hard, unsure if she'd dreamt it. But she was wide awake. How could a ghost be so lifelike? Was the child a ghost, or just another resident?

Determined, Sage returned to the photos, scanning through the earliest ones quickly. She tried to put the girl from her mind. Bella had merely lost her ribbon and slipped out. Sage also kept glancing at the lions, but no live eyes. Their stares remained blank. Though one looked like it had pushed further out from the mantle. A trick of the light? Sage bit on her lip. She couldn't let the manor get to her.

In the album, as she turned the pages, the sullen-sepia people changed to black-and-white. Then some pictures were in color, with smiling people leaning on old cars, or on board a yacht in the bay. Parties on the front lawn. Clothing became less formal.

One laughing woman in a long sheath dress and floppy hat had reddish-brown hair poking out from the brim. The same color as Bella's. Just a coincidence! Lawrence Brubaker, whom she'd seen in other pictures, stood close with a wide grin. The year was 1926, according to a scribbled note.

Unfortunately, there were no pictures of servants, except as vague figures in the background. So nothing to put Grandma Esther, in a clearer photo, on the estate. Of course, servants were invisible from what she'd read, and hardly deserved their pictures taken.

She turned another page and there was the same red-haired woman holding the handle of a baby carriage, her dress not as flashy or revealing. Sage then thought of what Bella had said about the 'others'. Wasn't that a movie? A movie about ghosts.

Besides, maybe, her Grandma Esther—still impossible to believe—who else crept spookily around this house?

Sage pulled out her phone to text Lilah. To take a picture of the library. But of course, no cell service.

Footsteps. She stuffed her phone away and turned to see Huntley had entered. He walked to the album. "Early color photos, very rare, and expensive."

"I guess the Brubakers didn't worry about money." She tried to sound, what had her mom called it, nonchalant?

"Did you find what you were looking for, Miss Emery?" His question seemed a challenge.

"Not really." She hadn't gone through all the 1920s, trying to track it by their clothing when no date was listed. She was confident she could tell the difference. "I need a few more minutes."

Huntley stared down at the album, at the red-haired woman. He wasn't moving away.

Sage cleared her throat. "Does a little girl named Bella Porter live here? I saw her a few minutes ago."

His eyes clouded. "There have been various visitors and relatives over the many years this house existed, including children."

Mr. Ever-evasive. Yet she wanted to like him but was unsure why. He had let her into the library to research.

But what about Bella? A hidden child? Or another strange vision. Sage palmed the side of her head. She began to think she was losing her mind. Still, Huntley didn't seem surprised she'd seen the child.

"I think you might know more than you say, sir." She fully faced him and kept her voice light.

He smirked, his gaze sharp again. "How old are you, Miss Emery?"

"I'll be fourteen in November." She stretched to her not-so-impressive height.

Huntley reached over and closed the album. He gave off the faint scent of a woodsy cologne. "A nice, innocent age."

No one was very innocent these days, she thought; not with the internet and social media. Plus, so many shootings; kids feared to attend school where they should be safe. And in September she'd be bussed off her island to high school. A whole different experience that excited her and made her nervous. Would she fit in?

"What's on the third floor?" she asked, unable to help herself.

"More empty rooms, discarded furniture, rolled-up carpets, those sorts of neglected things." He motioned for her to leave the library. Her research was over. "Hardly the place for curious young ladies."

Dare she tell him Bella had said her room was there? Was the child a neglected thing?

"Can I come back another time to look at the pictures?" Sage followed him out and he shut the door. She refused to be discouraged.

"Perhaps. However, too much knowledge can be unsettling, leading to unsafe situations. Be careful what you wish for." He opened the front door, and she felt thrown out by his words—though his tone sounded more concerned than dismissive.

* * *

Crickets chirred in the bushes when Sage leaned against a pine tree as the three of them stared across the clearing at Lakeluster House. The hour was late, too late. The moon rose in the oncoming night, reflected off the lake. This soon gave the house a glimmering sheen as the sky darkened and the reflection brightened.

48

"That's why it's called Lakeluster House," Sage said. Her dad had once brought them to see it, several years back. She admired the light caressing over the house's front. The shimmer gave the place a magical look, like a fairy tale. But what secrets did it hide? She clasped her sweater close.

"How would they know that when they built it?" Nate asked. "They weren't here in the dark, were they? Or did they change the name later?"

"It's stupid to name houses, anyway, bro. It has to be a joke on lackluster. More mysterious happenings." Patrick made a creepy *ooooh* sound. "Maybe Harrison Brubaker was a vampire and came here in the night, looking for people to bite and suck their blood." He flapped his hands near Nate's cheek.

"Stop it." Nate pushed him away. "You like being annoying."

"We shouldn't be here at all. Mom will have my head if she finds out." Sage sighed. She was just as guilty, her curiosity to view it again getting the best of her. She really wanted back in the library, to research any Porters. As in Bella.

"You already snuck out here *alone* to snoop yesterday." Patrick grimaced, his words snarky. "Uncle Ron took Aunt Jenny to a movie. A date night tonight. You should be happy about that."

"I am. And I was researching our great-great grandma. In the quiet, without boys." Sage was glad her parents spent more time together. Had they completely fixed their problems? Adults could be so confusing and secretive.

Something flapped out of a tree, then another. Bats? They circled near the manor as the luster faded.

"You shouldn't have gone without me. It was my idea to investigate in the first place." Patrick nudged her. "And you didn't find out anything. Did you ask to see the upper floors?"

She hadn't told them about Bella, or the shadowy woman with a gun. How long could she continue to hold back? She brought her cousin here to shut him up about her research trip. And here *she* was being secretive.

"I did ask, sort of. Huntley said it was all junk up there. We've seen the luster; time to go." Sage took a step into the trees, back toward town. "Before my parents come home." Were they enjoying themselves? She'd stressed herself for two years that her parents wouldn't end up in a divorce like Patrick's. They'd come so close. Now she felt queasy—parents, wobbly on their pedestals, gave her a headache.

Some creature howled in the distance. Probably one of the coyotes that roamed in these woods. Sage felt a prickle of discomfort.

"The reflection was awesome. The look of it." Nate shrugged, about to follow.

"That's not the only thing... Wait. *Look*." Patrick pointed, his voice raised.

Sage came back and stood beside her cousin at the wood's edge.

The front door of the manor had opened. A man in a long coat stepped out onto the porch. He had an old-fashioned hat pulled low. He swept to the left, his shadow flickering off the wall. Then he vanished, his shadow shifting into something ragged with claws as he melted into the edge of the porch.

Sage covered her mouth to stifle a yell as Nate gripped her arm. Patrick swore. Her heart racing, she didn't think the man was Huntley; he was too bulky and short. Whatever or whoever else occupied the manor?

* * *

Jacob:
It slid out again. The cursed creature. Was there someone in the woods worth exploring? Or chasing after? The beast is becoming too agitated. We don't need another horrible incident. No more police.

And the girl, Miss Emery. She is obstinate, eager to uncover the past. Should she be allowed? Or should she be protected? The child was here, too, in the library. I felt her presence. Bella...the poor waif. Miss Emery spoke to her, or at least saw her. Since she did see her, Miss Emery could be the special person connected to this place. Someone of the blood with a beating heart. Over a century has passed. Lakeluster has suffered enough; the time should come to end this travesty.

Chapter 6

Sage left the bakery on Nahant Road—the main road in their town—holding the cake meant for her dad's birthday. Her mom used to bake homemade cakes, like she did for Miss Dora, but so much had changed. Maybe too much, though things in her family seemed to be circling around again for the better.

Patrick and Nate followed, Nate munching on a free cupcake the owner had given him, crumbs covering his lips.

A seagull called in the ever-present briny breeze. Soon it would be July, and the area would be crowded with noisy tourists and their noisier cars.

"This town is so boring. No mall, no arcade. And everyone is beige flag. I can't wait for school and football practice in Hartford." Patrick thrust back his shoulders. He had gained muscle in the last couple of years. And he now stood half a head taller than her.

"Nahant is mostly homes, but you know that." Sage saw her cousin now preferred the city where he'd moved to in Connecticut, even with the eventual divorce. Those fun summer days when they were little kids—tag and hide and seek—were long over. "There aren't so many shops, except for the tourists."

Their shops were scattered among Victorian homes, smaller bungalows, and a large park with a gazebo. The historic district had some major stone buildings, including the columned newspaper office and the golden-stone public library. She took pride in those sturdy buildings. The public library! Would they have information on Lakeluster House and the murder?

"We do need an arcade." Nate munched more on his cupcake, icing smeared on his fingertips. "They used to have those old amusement parks."

"How is your mom, Aunt Theresa, doing?" Sage asked. "I wish she'd visit." Her aunt used to be a fun-loving, easy to laugh person. When she got together with Sage's mom, laughter filled the house.

"Her nursing job keeps her busy." Patrick spoke off-handedly, as if he really didn't want to go into details. "Shook! *They're* in town?" He elbowed her, almost causing her to drop the cake.

"Oww, I'm tired of you doing that," Sage protested. She'd poke him back if her hands weren't full. A kick to his shin? She looked where he indicated.

Across the road, near the Town Hall with its grand cupola, Huntley had exited a sleek, old-timey car, then assisted Miss Dora from the passenger side. The three children shrank back against the wall of the shop.

"Let's go. Mom's waiting." Sage gripped the box and could hardly look at the butler after what they'd seen two nights ago. Patrick swore he was a vampire (but did they have shadows?); Nate insisted on a werewolf. But was it even *him*? How could any of this be true? She'd tumbled into a fantasy story—caught between interest and, she had to admit it, fear.

Later that night, to calm Nate, she'd insisted it was only a trick of the reflection off the lake, but he hadn't believed her.

"Just think, bro. Now we can get into the house. It will be empty." Patrick, ever ready for mischief, grinned.

"Are you crazy? We'll be arrested for trespassing." Despite herself, she watched as Huntley and the lady entered a vintage clothing shop across the street.

Nate licked icing off his fingers after finishing the cupcake. "Sounds like it could be fun."

"I'm going. This is a dare. You losers can stay home." Patrick sprinted off down the street.

"*Wait.* We have to go after him." Sage turned to her brother, her breath rapid. "Or I do. You carry this cake to Mom. Please."

"Don't leave me out." Nate took the box, his frown deep. A dark lock of hair fell over his forehead. The cake shifted to one side. "You always leave me behind."

"Not true. Okay, sometimes. I'm going to stop Patrick, that's all. Before he ends up in juvie-jail." Sage clasped her brother's shoulders. She couldn't admit their mom warned her to look after him. "I have enough to worry about. Take the cake to Mom, and don't tell her anything."

Sage ran down the street, anger in her belly. Why did she have to be the cool head when it came to her cousin and brother?

* * *

Gulping for air, Sage reached the clearing before the manor after a one-mile dash through the woods suffering slaps of pine branches. Her fingers smelled like a Christmas tree. Her ankles ached; her combat boots weren't meant for long runs. Patrick was jiggling the front door. Then he left the porch and tried to lift the front windows.

"*Stop*, right now. They could come back any moment," Sage scolded as she approached. "What's the matter with you?"

"Oh, stop being such a girl. I want excitement." He rounded the corner of the manor.

Sage followed, her face hot. She'd once prided herself on being as brave as any boy.

Patrick had jerked open a side window, paint flaking off the frame. He pushed it up with a screech of wood.

"Please don't do it. I'll have to tell my parents." She rushed to him and grabbed his leg in his jeans as he hoisted himself up.

"Let *go*." He kicked her grasp off and wriggled inside. She heard a thump. "I'll open the front door for you. Explore with me."

Disgusted, shaking with frustration, she clenched her fists and hurried back to the porch. The door clicked and squeaked. Patrick pulled it open.

She marched up the steps to him. "You'll be arrested, you idiot."

He grabbed her hand and dragged her inside. "Let's run to the third floor. We won't take long."

"No!" She jerked away from him. "This is stupid."

But he was already across the room and mounting the elegant staircase.

She snatched out her phone, hoping for a miracle, but still no service. No way to call her mom. She raced after him.

"Come back before we're both in trouble," she pleaded, but he ignored her. The dim house closed in around her as she rushed up the stairs and down the upper hall. Her heartbeat thundered.

"There has to be another staircase." Patrick opened a door at the end of the hall. "Here it is."

She reached him and stared at a shadowed set of stairs that seemed to narrow as they rose. He clomped up them as if to ward off any doubts.

"You'd better be quick." She started up and cringed when a cobweb crawled over her face. She swept it aside. "You have no idea what might be there. I've seen things. Other then the night on the porch."

Patrick hesitated on the landing, brow knitted. "What things?"

Sage crowded next to him and opened the door onto a narrow hall draped in shadow. "You won't believe me. I hardly believe it myself."

"Are you gonna tell me or not?" He pushed past her into the hall.

The musty smell was overpowering. Her lungs felt full of dust. She coughed.

"No, I'm not." If she told him, it would only increase his interest, his craziness.

"You're lying." His laugh grated on her. "You've nothing more to tell. That shapeshifter on the porch was cool enough. Though it was blurry. Kinda fuzzy."

Blurry? Fuzzy? It had appeared sharp as anything to Sage. She decided to keep that to herself. Patrick might need glasses.

He opened a few doors. "Junk, furniture; oh, here's a child's bed with a doll on it."

Sage joined him at that door. Bella's room? She stepped in. A window on the back wall gave scant light through drab curtains. The metal-framed bed was neatly made with a colorful quilt. The doll, her russet ringlets dangling over a yellow dress, stared up with blue eyes in her porcelain face. A crack in one cheek gave her a creepy look, the eyes too bright.

Shadows and dust filled the small chamber. A dresser on the other side had a hairbrush and a carved wooden box of ribbons. Sage breathed slowly. Bella could be real and not a ghost. But for some reason, Huntley wanted to keep her a secret. Still, why so much dust in an occupied room?

Sounds of rummaging in the next room caught her attention. She found Patrick digging through cushions, rolled carpets, and old clothes. A rickety rocking chair sat in a corner. Sage half-expected it to rock by itself.

"Why are you so hyper? We have to go. *Now*." She thrust her hands on her hips.

He stood and glared at her. "My mom called this morning. Dad is marrying that bitch he left us for. She's half his age."

"Oh, no." Sage slumped against the wall. Her stomach pinched. "I'm so sorry."

"I'll never speak to him again. He's cancelled." He continued his rampage through the discarded junk, opening drawers in an old highboy.

Sage didn't know what to say about that. She almost reminded him of her own father's brief straying. And Sage remained leery around him. Their closeness damaged.

She felt both betrayals. Her jovial Uncle Steve, a loud guy to be honest, with his sweep of wavy blonde hair. A California surfer, her mom once called him; a physician's assistant originally from Los Angeles, he loved to flirt and tease. How handsome he'd looked beside her aunt, a slim dark-blonde with a lovely smile. Was she still smiling now? Sage's world felt unsteady, swaying beneath her feet.

"Okay, you might change your mind later about your dad. Adults do what they want and don't ask us for permission. But we need to leave before we're caught." A noise from the hallway made her step from the room. Nothing was there, the shadows deeper. A chill suddenly enveloped her as an icy finger touched the back of her neck.

Chapter 7

Sage whipped about and caught a gauzy shape flitting across the wood-paneled wall. Then the wall appeared to ripple. She struggled to take an even breath.

A shadow in the corner moved, then raised long arms, its hands morphing into claws. Sage gulped, but any sound or cry clogged her throat. A giant scratch appeared on the panel beside the claw. Sage felt like a darkness coated over her, weighing on her flesh. She thrust out her hands as if to push it away. The shadow lengthened into a thin, tall tree shape, then the thing scrunched up like a hunchback. Next the shadow folded into itself and slithered through the wall.

Air gushed from her lungs, and she almost stumbled. Was that the shapeshifter?

Down at the other end of the hall, the woman she'd seen before drifted into view, mostly transparent, holding the pistol against her chest.

Sage opened her mouth to call her cousin, feeling she could now, but something in the woman's expression begged her to be quiet. Sage forced herself to step toward the vision. The woman's eyes grew huge, the same hazel color as Sage's.

"Are you my Great-Great grandmother Esther?" Sage whispered. Suddenly, she could no longer move, her feet frozen to the floor.

A second shape joined the woman. A young man with golden-brown hair and piercing blue eyes. He held up his hands as if in surrender or to make excuses. He resembled a younger version of Huntley. A relative? An ancestor?

The two ghosts glanced her way, their forms wavering like a breeze blew through them.

Sage gasped; a tiny cry escaped. The figures dissolved into the air. Panic crawled through her veins from both incidents.

"What are you doing?" Patrick's voice shattered the following silence.

Her body hummed like a tuning fork. She turned to frown at him. "Did you see anything? No? We're leaving. Right now."

"I'm looking for a trapdoor to the attic." He stared up at the ceiling. "I'm amped now. This should be mad."

She marched back and grabbed his arm. "Come with me, or I'm returning home to tell my mom to call your mom. Do you understand?"

He stared at her as if she'd lost her mind. Which was possible. With a muttered curse, he said, "okay, this time. But I want to come back."

Sage hauled him down the hall to the stairs. The ugly scratch remained on the wall. "Only if we're invited. Hopefully they won't catch us today."

She wanted to return, too, to further her research, but she couldn't get the two ghostly figures, and the creepy shadow, out of her head. Her brain felt on fire.

* * *

Mom and Sage stood on the front porch with its glimpse of the red-roofed church in the setting sun. The porch had been added later to their little house. A cunning woman (the same as a healer suspected of witchcraft) was rumored to have lived here in colonial times. Luckily, she'd escaped the Salem Witch trials by a few decades. But many still called it the witch's house.

Sage sipped her hot chocolate, the rich flavor soothing. Even though it was almost summer, she still enjoyed the drink. "Did you hear Uncle Steve is marrying his girlfriend?"

Mom drank from her chocolate and grimaced. "Theresa called me. She's trying not to let it upset her. I mean, we all figured he would."

"Patrick is angry." Sage swirled the last of the chocolate in her cup.

"That's natural. We must be kind and care about his situation." Mom turned to study her. "How does it make you feel?"

"Sorry for him. He's gotten so restless. Annoying, and looking to get into trouble." Sage leaned on the porch rail. "I feel disappointed. I guess angry, too. Uncle Steve hurt Aunt Theresa and his family."

Mom's gaze turned sad. She took another drink. "I've meant to ask. Is there more you want to discuss? Concerning our family?"

Sage hesitated. "We've never talked about it. About Dad."

"I thought you were too young at the time. Now, what do you know?" Mom's voice came out wistful.

"Dad had a...girlfriend, when I was eleven." She practically whispered it through a tightening throat. Had Nate noticed? He'd been only nine.

"An affair, yes." Mom pursed her lips, and her eyes narrowed. "It's hard to trust someone after that, though he swore it didn't mean anything."

Sage thought of the pain inside her when she looked at her dad. People weren't who you thought they were. They harbored dark secrets. Where she'd once sought comfort in his hugs and wide lap, she now saw him as too different, too ready to desert them—like Patrick's dad.

"It seems men like to be loved by more than one woman. Selfish." Sage fought the urge to hug her mom. To bury her face in her chest like a little girl. "Uncle Steve did like to flirt with women. I saw it."

"Not all men are like that." Mom gave her a half-smile, though it didn't soften her eyes. "My father doted on my mother. I am trying to forgive your father completely, but it's a process. You should, too."

"I don't think I'll ever get married." Boys, then men, were too wild, danger-loving, and disloyal in her opinion. She planned to take care of herself.

"People never behave like you wish they would. It's a hard truth." Jenny sighed and finished her drink. "Your father swore it never...went beyond a few kisses. Oh, I shouldn't have told you that." She leaned close to her. "We're always here for you. You know that?"

"I do." But could they believe Dad about the affair? She glanced at her mom, suddenly wanting to tell her about what she'd seen at Lakeluster House, but her parents might send her to a counselor for being mental. The visions today had really unsettled her. Was the young man the valet who'd been shot? The one her Grandma Esther supposedly loved. And what about his resemblance to Huntley? Had she imagined the similar features?

In her room, after washing her face and pulling on her pajamas, she texted Lilah. *We have to meet tomorrow. I have a ghost story to tell.*

Sage patted the powder over Lilah's already beautiful complexion. She used the lightest tone. Then she leaned in and applied brown eye shadow, feathering it with her fingers to give her the smoky eye, although it was almost out of fashion.

"Do you believe you really saw those things?" Lilah asked as she fidgeted in the chair in Sage's bedroom. "Scary. It hardly seems real."

"I swear I did." Or was it all in her head? Did insanity run in her family? But Bella had seemed so solid, a living person. Perhaps she *was* and Huntley wouldn't admit she lived there. But why? "Do you want to come with me and see if you discover anything?"

"We are close to Salem, and you live in your witchy house. Ghost stories everywhere. Lakeluster was always said to be haunted." Lilah shrugged, though her gaze looked disturbed. "Do I want to go? No, I don't like hauntings. Ghosts with guns. It'll be our secret."

Sage carefully applied black eye liner to Lilah's eyelids, making a forked tail at the end of each one to give an exotic appearance. "I'm finding it fascinating, though creepy as hell."

"You're braver than me. Can I open my eyes?" Lilah did so. She looked in the mirror on the white vanity table. "Nice."

"Would you like a butterfly or a snake on your cheek?" Sage smirked into her reflection. She hadn't felt brave yesterday.

"Oh, a butterfly, girl." Lilah preened. "You know I like pretty things."

"You'll have all the boys chasing after you in high school." Sage brushed back her dark bangs with her wrist.

"Mom says I'm too young for boys. But I'll be fourteen in September." Lilah laughed. "And dad being in the military, he'll fire a tank on any boys."

"Your dad's in the navy. More like a ship's torpedo. Sit still." Sage used the eyeliner pen to outline a butterfly on her friend's cheek in careful strokes. "We should buy false eyelashes. That's what all the big actresses wear."

"And they usually look like giant spiders crouch on their faces." Lilah batted her eyes. "Mom would kill me if she saw that."

Sage opened a tiny case of purple, sparkly eye shadow in a paste. Perfect to create the inside of the butterfly wings. Here, in her room, everything seemed so normal.

A knock on her door startled her. She'd grown too jumpy lately.

"Who is it?"

The door opened and Nate poked his head in. "Hey, I found an old article, well only half a year old, about your teacher, Mr. Saunders."

"What did it say?" Sage asked, her interest piqued.

"A big announcement he was going to write a book on the history of Lakeluster House." Nate sounded proud of his investigative skills. "He even had a book deal."

"He did mention the book in class once," Lilah said. "Poor man."

"Anything else?" Sage prodded. "Was he interviewing people who used to live there?"

"Yeah, he spoke to that butler Huntly we met, the article said." Nate nodded. "But he had just moved in and said he didn't know much about the history."

"I find that hard to believe. Then Mr. Saunders was murdered." Sage shivered. "Someone didn't want the history to be written." And killed in such a gross way, like a werewolf had torn him up—the creature they'd seen on the front porch! And the shadow in the hallway.

"The police still have no suspects, I guess." Lilah frowned as she applied an apricot gloss to her lips.

"None that we *know* of," Sage replied. Had Huntley and Miss Dora moved into the house to prevent anyone from discovering its secrets? Yet they'd allowed them in. Was there a reason behind that? Plus, the house had been empty for decades. Or had it?

"I'll look for more stuff." Nate rolled his eyes, muttering about their make-up, then backed out and shut the door.

Sage scraped a brush through the purple paste to steady her thoughts. She should stay away from the manor, but something drew her to it, like a pull of many threads. But could they bind her to a dangerous place? She must be very careful with a clawed shadow and ghostly lovers roaming about. Surely she hadn't imagined them. And how to keep Patrick under control?

"What's the matter? You look extra troubled." Lilah watched her in the mirror.

Sage forced a laugh to chase away the creeps. "My life is just so high key."

Chapter 8

In the room off the kitchen, at a small round table, Huntley set the steaming teapot on the trivet. Miss Dora sliced up a yellow cake drizzled in sugary frosting and passed the delicate plates around.

As they sat down with Miss Dora, Sage couldn't help glancing at Huntley, thinking of the male ghost she saw upstairs. A younger, thinner apparition that reminded her of him. She swallowed, hard. Had 'viewing' ghosts become the norm for her?

Nate dug into his cake. Patrick took small bites, his look distracted.

Their break-in had been two days before. Yesterday they had tried to visit—at Patrick's insistence—but were told to come back today for tea.

"What exactly is your attachment to the house?" Miss Dora asked, her smile sweet.

"Our great-great grandma worked here," Patrick blurted.

"She was a housekeeper, probably when Lawrence Brubaker was in charge. The 1920s." Sage poured milk into her tea until it turned a beige color. She hoped she didn't sound nervous, putting the details out there.

"Her name was Esther Collins," Nate said, his mouth half-full.

Huntley arched his eyebrows, his gaze on them stern. "Are you certain about that?"

Sage felt a sudden chill coming from him. Yet why did it seem that he already knew this? She squirmed in her chair. "Yes, very certain."

"There was a murder," Patrick said with too much gusto.

Huntley glanced at Miss Dora, whose eyes sharpened for a second, before she reverted to her fuzzy expression.

Sage wanted to kick her cousin under the table. But in her proper dress, as her mom said she should be, she strained to act lady-like.

"I found it on the internet." Nate sipped his tea, then added more sugar.

"But our family already knew," Patrick retorted.

"Oh my, what is an internet?" Miss Dora cocked her head, her smile and watery gaze curious. Today she wore a paisley dress with lace at the collar, as if she tried to look younger than she was.

Sage ate a bite of cake, a moist vanilla flavor, the frosting sweet. Were these people so stuck in the past, they knew nothing of the internet? "Nate can explain."

"It's a huge network. It connects you to places all over the world. I can talk to people in England, and France if they speak English." Nate grinned. "You need a computer, or cell phone."

"With a connection that you pay for with a provider." Sage ate and drank slowly, watching everyone.

A sideboard against the far wall held two small greenish stone lions, who stared back at her. Would their eyes come alive like the ones on the mantel in the library? Sage clutched the napkin in her lap.

"With a cable, phone-line, or dish," Nate added.

"Mercy. That internet sounds too complicated for me." Miss Dora sipped her tea, pinky pointed.

"Our Grandma Esther was supposed to have shot another servant. Isn't that eerie?" Patrick laughed, but his eyes narrowed as he obviously fished for information. "She killed him."

Huntley, who'd stood nearby as if on guard, poured more tea in quick, nearly sloppy actions.

"That was the rumor, but it wasn't proven." Sage wondered what had disturbed the butler. Was it *his* ancestor who was killed? He always seemed to know more than he admitted. "Our two-greats grandmother left Nahant for years after that."

"This house has such a rich history." Miss Dora took a dainty bite of cake. "But a murder? Have we heard of that, Huntley?"

"There are many legends about Lakeluster House." Huntley's reply sounded as though he pretended to be dismissive.

"Did you have relatives who worked here, back in the 1920s, Mr. Huntley?" Sage couldn't stop herself from asking.

Huntley stiffened, his chin raised. "It's possible. My family has been in service for many years, even here in America. We've served diplomats and traveled the world."

"But Huntley never married. He devoted himself to my service. His father served my father." Miss Dora nodded.

Sage caught a flash of resentment on Huntley's face, but he quickly smoothed out his expression.

"You must love flowers." Nate finished his cake, indicating the floral wallpaper that covered this room's walls. Yellow and pink blooms with twisting green stems.

"The Victorians wallpapered everything," Huntley said dryly.

"And my ancestors never changed it." Miss Dora pouted as if to forgive them. A child-like woman? Someone who lived in a rosy haze? While Sage felt on the edge of growing up and becoming a woman, whether she liked it or not. Why did this house feel like a step in that direction?

"What's a Victorian?" Nate eyed the cake as if he wanted more.

"That's what they call this architecture, the American version being very ornate, and the people who lived then, during the reign of Queen Victoria of England. Roughly between 1837 and 1901." Huntley's words droned out.

"Can we have another tour of the house?" Patrick leaned back in his chair, noticeably impatient for the party to end.

This time, Sage nudged his shin with her foot. "Where did you live before moving into the manor, Miss Dora?"

"Oh, in England. But in a remote village in the countryside." The woman sliced another piece of cake. Nate held up his plate, and she placed the slice on it.

"Do you have any family left?" Sage finished her cake but waved off a second piece.

"No one close, I'm afraid. I might be the last of the direct line to Harrison Brubaker." Miss Dora's expression took on a dreamy quality, though again she always seemed only half-present to Sage. "I was a sheltered girl with doting parents. I cared for them in their last years, so had little time to meet an appropriate beau."

"What's a bo?" Nate asked.

"A gentleman caller," Huntly said.

"A boyfriend," Sage replied. Her parents must have been ill for many years to discourage boys. Of course, in the old days older women didn't attract men, her mom once said. They didn't have the great face creams women had now.

Patrick tapped his fork on his plate. "My cousin's teacher was found hanged from the tree near the pond."

"Patrick!" Sage scowled at him. "This isn't the time." He'd promised her he would behave. She should have known better.

Miss Dora covered her mouth, her gaze flitting around the room. A pink hue bloomed on her cheeks. "That can't be true."

"That is an inappropriate subject, young man," Huntley scolded, but didn't appear shocked by the information. He snatched the teapot and entered the kitchen.

"I apologize, Miss Dora," Sage said. "My cousin needs better manners."

Patrick glared at her but said nothing.

Nate gobbled up his second piece of cake, frosting on his lips. Sage prayed he wouldn't bring up the rumor that Mr. Saunders had been skinned like a rabbit—if that was really true.

"I try to ignore the bad things in the world," Miss Dora said with a sigh. "Patrick, you have quite an imagination."

"Bad things find you no matter what." Patrick finished the last of his cake, his expression now gloomy. He obviously thought of his father's betrayal toward his mother.

Huntley returned with another hot pot of tea. He poured Miss Dora a second cup.

"Huntley, didn't we have a visitor shortly after we moved here? He said he was a historian who wanted to write about the house?" Miss Dora brushed her left hand through her hair, and her fingers came away bloody...then the blood vanished.

Sage's cake churned in her stomach. No one else reacted.

"Miss Dora, what happened to—?" Sage began.

"I slightly recall that visitor, Miss." Huntley held up the pot, but the rest of them declined. His look at Sage silenced her, but she didn't understand why.

She stared at the woman's hand again; it remained clean. Then she wondered since they lived here at the time, how could they not be aware of the murder? Didn't the police investigate? Or had Huntley sheltered Miss Dora from the whole thing? Sage rubbed her knees, her mind racing.

Light, quick footsteps sounded overhead. Sage looked up, the hair on the back of her neck prickling. Then she glanced at the rest of them. Again, no one appeared to have noticed. Except for Huntley, who stared right at her as if daring her to mention it.

"We should go. Thank you for the tea and cake." Sage rose, unsettled. Was that a ghost, other people who lived here, or didn't live at all?

Patrick stood. "Can we come back to explore your fine house?" His words came out even and polite, to Sage's surprise.

"You've seen much of the house already, I daresay." Huntley arched an eyebrow as though he knew about their break-in.

"I enjoyed it, the tea and the cake." Nate scraped back his chair. "Thank you."

"And I enjoyed your company. Yes, do come again." Miss Dora remained seated, her small hands folded on the table. The light in the room changed, leaving a red slash on Miss Dora's head, like blood—the same place where her fingers had been. Sage's breath froze.

"I'll show you out." Huntley gestured in the direction of the front door.

The three of them followed him. Sage tried to understand what she saw. She glanced over when they passed the staircase. The doll with the cracked cheek sat on the third step as if watching them. Her pulse jumped. Had Bella left it there?

Chapter 9

Sage sat down at a computer terminal in the public library and accessed the library archives on newspapers. After much searching, *The Boston Globe* had an article on the shooting at Lawrence Brubaker's manor house on Nahant.

"A manservant by the name of Jacob Huntley was found shot on the upper floor of Lakeluster House." Sage sucked in her breath as she whispered the words. Huntley. He had to be an ancestor of the current butler, another secret revealed. No wonder the ghost she'd seen resembled him.

She read on: "No one confessed to the murder, but the housekeeper, Mrs. Esther Collins, was rumored to be in a romantic relationship with the young man. Nothing was ever proven that she had anything to do with the murder. The investigation continues." The date was 1925.

Sage sat back in the chair, thoughts tumbling. She strained to wipe bloody fingers from her memory. Why was she, and it seemed Huntley, the only ones who noticed?

The library was quiet with few people perusing the books. *Perusing*; her friends often teased her for her fancy words. A girl who'd always loved to read, she hadn't read much lately. The clean smell of paper pleased her. The large blond furniture, rectangular room with shelves and posters, had a children's corner where once Sage and Nate had come to enjoy story time, before the messy world of adults intruded.

She leaned forward and typed in the name Bella Porter.

Another article came up after several minutes. Not as clear as the first. Older and yellowed. "A relative of Harrison Brubaker reported her daughter, Bella Porter, had gone missing from Lakeluster House. A child, neither she nor her body were ever found."

She looked at the date. Bella was born in the 1800s? Sage trembled. The child seemed so real that day in the manor library. And the doll left on the stairs. The house was full of creepy events. How could she believe them? She should never return and forget she ever met these people.

Sage massaged her forehead and powered down the computer.

Yet she wanted to find out more. The mystery had taken over her waking hours.

Huntley seemed the answer to her questions, though he always evaded her. Miss Dora played the feather-headed owner, but did she know more? Why was her head wounded—and then it vanished?

And what if Sage proved her great-great grandmother was the killer? Her family would probably be angry with her.

She didn't know which way to turn. She brought out her phone and texted Lilah. *I need to talk to you. When can we meet?*

* * *

"I'm all open to the supernatural, especially after visits to spooky Salem during Halloween, but this sounds pretty bizarre." Lilah watched Sage closely to see if she joked.

They stood on the cliffs again, the bay swirling below. The tourist boats were accumulating in the harbor. Fancy craft, some motored, some with sails. Beer cans already littered the beaches. The warming air as June slipped to July would soon be muggy with humidity.

"It's the truth, girl. I talked to this child. She was wearing granny clothes." Sage swiped her hair aside, picturing Bella. Their strange conversation.

"Maybe that was another Bella, a descendant." Lilah placed her hands on the hips of her ripped jeans. Her pink crop top fit her slender form perfectly.

Sage wore a blouse with thin vertical stripes which would elongate her body, her mom had said. She'd hoped to grow a few more inches, but it looked doubtful now. Five foot one might be her fate. "No one says the kid even lives or lived there." Huntley wouldn't admit it anyway. And Sage somehow couldn't mention the blood incident. The more she stewed on it, the more she convinced herself she imagined the whole thing.

A red sports car convertible zoomed by with a load of loud tourists whooping it up. The invaders that kept Nahant going, Sage mused.

Lilah eyed her again. "Maybe you shouldn't go back. It could be…"

"Dangerous?" Sage shrugged and inhaled the salty breeze. Why did that possibility suddenly thrill her? "I thought about that, but I'm too into it now."

"Be careful. And the butler… He looks like the ghost you say you actually saw?" Lilah leaned close, her whisper drawn out.

"Yes! A younger version. A guy my Grandma Esther was supposed to be in love with. He had to be a relative of Huntley." Another thing he probably wouldn't admit to.

"You think she killed him, as the paper said, or suspected?"

"Allegedly. She was holding a pistol both times I saw her. If that was my Grandma Esther." Sage fought a cringe. "You can't tell anyone about this."

"Who would believe me? But you know I wouldn't. Are you sure they aren't putting meth in your tea over there?"

Sage laughed. "They'd better not. I don't touch drugs, you silly. But I'm not sure of anything anymore."

"You never told me you could see ghosts before." Was Lilah growing skeptical? Sage couldn't blame her if she was.

"I didn't know it." Sage wasn't certain she liked this new talent, but it did make things interesting. "I'm still trying to understand who sees what when."

"Yeah, a lot to unpack. Have you talked with our village witch, Mrs. Crippin?" Lilah grinned, as if forcing herself to be helpful. "She might know the history."

"Is she for real?" Sage scoffed. The old woman ran a shop called Witchy Wiles, where she sold potions, perfumes, and candles. And souvenirs. "Most people think she's a fake."

Two boys rode by on their bicycles. They whistled and hooted.

The girls waved at them, Lilah with more enthusiasm. Sage wondered at her disinterest in boys. Had her dad's actions soured her? Or the urge hadn't kicked in yet.

"Hey, I'm trying out for the play the high school is supposed to be performing this year. *Grease*, of all things." Lilah fluffed her blonde hair. "I'd make the perfect Sandy."

Sage resented being pulled back to the here and now. "I'll help with your make-up. Did you hear if Mr. Saunders's daughter is back for the summer?"

"I think so. She likes to visit her mom. I'm surprised her mom still lives here after Mr. Saunders's murder." Lilah sighed. "Such a good teacher."

"Let's try to talk to her. Maybe she knows more about what happened." Sage started to walk away from the cliff.

"If she'll talk to us. She's eighteen and at that bougie college." Lilah stuck up her nose and followed. "Harvard." As the middle child in a large family, Lilah would have to find scholarships for her to attend college.

"We can only try." Sage linked arms with her friend. She wanted to gather more clues, a detective on the job. Instead of enjoying her last summer before high school, her mind was too tangled up with Lakeluster house. And why was she taking the idea of ghosts so easily—instead of hiding under her bed? Of course, she'd never been a sissy girl. This felt like a video game she had to solve, or win. The challenge drove her on and skimmed over the possibility of risk.

Chapter 10

Sage and Lilah sat on the front porch steps of a light blue Victorian cottage across from the park with the huge gazebo. On the fourth of July they often had music there. Then the beer-guzzling, hot dog eating tourists who attended trashed the lawn.

Christine Saunders, her large breasts pushing against her red-flowered tank top, leaned against the porch post, her auburn hair pulled back in a ponytail. Her cut-offs showed shapely legs. She glared at them both. "What do you want to know, and why?"

"My family is part of the manor's history," Sage replied.

"History. That's what got my dad killed." Christine scoffed. "He wanted to write a book on the history of Lakeluster House. I wish that decrepit pile would burn down."

"Do you think someone wanted him *not* to write it?" Lilah asked.

"Clearly." Christine picked at her fingernail, brow furrowed in her round, pretty face. "He interviewed a man who was supposed to know about the history, the murder, the other strange happenings."

"Like missing children?" Sage shifted on the hard wooden step. She kept her voice soft, so as not to further irritate the older girl.

"My great-great grandmother was involved in that murder. Did you know that?"

"I learned more about it from Dad." Christine's eyes clouded for an instant. "I'm surprised he didn't interview your grandmother before she died."

"He might've tried. Grandma Jean never wanted to talk about the past." Sage hid her disappointment that people liked to cling to their privacy. To her mind, only the guilty hid those details.

"Well, I wish he'd stayed away from all of it. We moved here ten years ago, because Dad liked the area. A wild almost-an-island, he called it. Plus his teaching job. We should've stayed in Delaware. Dad would still be alive." Christine chewed on her lower lip and swished her ponytail like a...pony. "God, I hate this place. But my mother is reluctant to move. I hope when I'm done with college she will." She tapped her long fingernails that had tiny roses painted on them on her thigh. "My dad might have spoken to your mom."

"My mom has never said." Sage wondered if she'd kept that from her. She needed to find out.

"What about this man he talked to. Who was he?" Lilah asked the question before Sage could.

"I don't remember. It's probably in Dad's notes on his computer." Christine sighed. "How can you stand it here? It's suffocating. The same people, except in the summer. No nightlife. I'm so relieved to live in Boston at Harvard."

She'd gotten a scholarship through academics was the story.

"I wouldn't mind Boston," Lilah said, her glossy blonde hair lying perfectly on her shoulders and down her back. "But I'm planning on New York, Broadway."

"Have the police looked at your dad's notes to find out about the man?" Sage straightened. She wouldn't mind living in a more exciting place herself. Though Lakeluster House had recently made her life intriguing.

"I'm sure they have. For what good they've done." Christine flipped up her hands. "No suspects so far. They should bring in more sophisticated police."

A kid chasing a scruffy dog ran past the porch. The noisy, increased traffic zoomed down the road.

"Can we see the notes?" Sage gave her a hopeful smile.

Christine pushed away from the post. "You should stay out of this. Do you want to end up like my dad? Don't be stupid. You're too young. I hate bothering with any of it when nothing happens." She entered the house, slamming the screen door. Then she popped back out. "I just remembered. My dad referred to the man with the initials J. H. The police asked me if I knew such a person. But don't waste time trying to solve it. You're just kids." She slipped back inside.

"She's a happy one." Lilah stood, brushing off her jeans. "Though she did lose her dad in that gross way."

"That would be hard. I'd love to see those notes." Sage rose, thoughts dancing over the possibilities. Why did Christine give them a clue yet warn them off? "But how to get to the computer?"

J. H.? Jacob Huntley? The murdered man and her Grandma Esther's rumored lover? That would be impossible. Or had the current butler the same initials? He had mentioned, briefly, that he was the one Mr. Saunders had spoken to. Plus an article Nate found confirmed it.

* * *

Huntley stared down at Sage on the manor's front porch. Patrick and Nate hovered behind her. "What may I do for you today, Miss Emery?"

"I'd like to look at your photo albums again." She tried her most winning smile. After yesterday's talk with Christine Saunders, she ached to know more about this man before her—but must make it look like a research project. Of course, she could end up hanging from a tree near the lake. And what about the creeping shadow they'd seen that night on this very porch? Her scalp prickled.

Huntley raised his chin. "And you brought your motley crew?"

"We insisted on coming," Patrick said.

Patrick had followed her when she left the house, then Nate had run after them.

"I told the crew to stay home, but boys never take orders well." She suppressed her annoyance at their intrusion.

Huntley nearly smiled at that. He wore a maroon vest with gold buttons, a white linen scarf tied neatly around his neck. Very old-school, her mom would say.

"Then I'll be indulgent. Please come in. Miss Dora might consent to seeing you later." Huntley opened the door wider. "Don't make too much noise."

Sage entered, the boys on her heels. The butler showed them to the library. The pleasant wood smell filled Sage's nose.

"Wow, so many books!" Nate exclaimed. "Do you have any about computers?"

"I doubt it. Most of these books are from an earlier time." Huntley went to the shelf with the albums and pulled them out, laying them on the desk.

Patrick picked up the handcuffs from the small table. "Do you have a dungeon? People chained to walls?"

"Put those down, young man. They are an antique," Huntley warned. Then he narrowed his eyes. "Wall-chains could be arranged."

Sage tried to ignore her cousin. She opened one of the albums, releasing the musty scent, and thought of Bella who had come up behind her in this room. Would she ever see her again? She pondered why these 'ghosts' showed themselves to her and not the boys. A shiver ran up her spine. "Mr. Huntley, can I ask you a question?"

"You may ask. I may not answer." He folded his hands in front of him, his words a dare. He watched her closely with his penetrating blue eyes.

"What is your first name?"

"And why would you need that information?" He said it nicely, his head tilted.

Patrick was at the fireplace mantel, poking around the carved lions' heads, near the now dead eyes that once stared at her. Maybe one would bite him.

Nate surveyed the names on the books on the many shelves.

"I found the murder victim in an old article at the public library. His name was Jacob Huntley. Was he a relative of yours?" She winced when his gaze turned sharp, like blue spears.

"Perhaps." He pointed a finger. "Be careful where you snoop around, my dear."

"I'm sorry if I was rude." Yet he'd allowed them in here, as if he couldn't make up his mind about how much they should discover. Or was there something more sinister? The man seemed to thrive on being deliberately mysterious.

"I must check on Miss Dora." He bowed his head like an old-fashioned butler in those historical shows her mom enjoyed on public television. "I will leave you to it."

He left the library.

"I'm shocked he didn't throw us out." Patrick grinned with a one shoulder shrug.

"So am I." Sage slowly flipped the pages of the album to the 1920s, where she'd left off before. Huntley was a puzzle, and she *had* to find out more. She kept discounting the idea of danger. This was an adventure that made her pulse trip. Her breath hitched. She had become as reckless as Patrick, but for different reasons.

Patrick returned to the handcuffs and began to closely inspect them.

"Put them down, please," Sage insisted. How much would she accomplish with these two messing about?

Nate came over to the fireplace. "Those lions look like they could jump off from here." He traced his fingers over the lions—would one start to growl? He touched other carvings on the mantal then a crest between two lions. A family crest, Sage wondered?

"The lions in the carving look ferocious," Patrick said, sidling over. He pressed on the crest. "It moves!"

"Just like a button," Nate said in amazement.

Patrick pushed his thumbs harder into the crest.

A creaking noise started and grew louder.

A panel beside the fireplace popped open an inch. Nate stepped back, eyes huge. Patrick yelped in excitement and pulled at the edge. Sage wanted to object, but the words stuck in her throat.

The panel opened like a door at Patrick's efforts. Darkness hung behind it. A secret passage, like in a spooky movie.

Chapter 11

Sage's stomach plunged at the narrow black expanse. Nate grabbed her arm and she twinged.

Patrick snatched out his phone and turned on the tiny flashlight. "This is awesome. I'm going to explore, bro."

Sage would usually have warned him, but this time her curiosity about this house pushed her to join in. "I hope Huntley doesn't catch us." Then she turned to Nate, the boy her mom said to always protect. "Stay out here and keep watch."

"No. I'm going too." Her brother pinched his lips. "I want to know what's in there. Don't try to stop me."

Sage sighed and pulled out her phone. She switched on the flashlight. "Then keep beside me."

Patrick stepped into the dark passage, swinging the tiny point of light around. The walls looked painted black, the floor black wood.

"I wonder if this had a purpose, like the Underground Railroad we learned about in school." Sage slowly followed, her skin prickling. Were runaway slaves snuck through here, hidden from the southerners out to catch them?

Nate kept at her shoulder. The darkness shrouded them both. The air smelled moldy.

"Patrick, slow down," she hissed at her cousin. His point of light had dimmed in front of them.

As she walked, she thought of haunted houses set up on Halloween. Would rattling skeletons and jerking ghosts jump out at them? Both so stupidly fake. What might jump out here that wasn't fake? She strained to calm her breath.

The walls seemed to widen then narrow, shifting in her light. Was it a trick of the dark? She'd begun to think she had too wild an imagination.

"What if this goes on forever?" Nate asked.

"It has to lead somewhere," Patrick said, his enthusiasm sharp. His footsteps remained too brisk.

Strings like spider webs swept against her face. Sage flinched, swiped them aside, and kept walking, slow and steady. Surely they had to reach an end, another door. In her sweep of light, she caught something white, high on the wall. A blinking eye? More than one? She focused her beam, but nothing was there now. Her hand shook.

"Here's a door." Patrick stopped a few yards ahead.

Sage increased her pace to reach him. The hall had lengthened, stretching, a crazy sight or not, and she couldn't see him. Then the darkness seemed to close in on her, thickening, like a wool coat.

A sudden burst of cold sliced into her. She shivered. "Did you feel that?" she asked Nate.

"No? What?" He'd slowed, his voice sounding faraway.

"Keep up with me," she warned. Sage stopped and raised her light; the hall appeared to curve. She couldn't see Patrick anywhere. She was about to call out for her cousin. Something materialized in front of her, shifting hues of white and beige, transparent, yet slightly solid.

She froze, mute, unable to turn her head to see if Nate was there. Alarm rushed through her.

The woman in the long apron morphed out of the floating material. She turned her pleading eyes on Sage. "He no longer loved me," she murmured. "We had plans."

"Grandma Esther?" Sage thought she said the words aloud, or were they in her head? Had she really heard the woman speak?

The young man who resembled Huntley in a thinner version appeared beside the woman. "It was over, Essie," he said with a British accent. 'We had a bit of fun. Let's remain friends."

Sage's stomach tightened into a fist. Why couldn't *she* speak?

The man then stared right at Sage, his eyes black holes, which suddenly changed to ice blue. "Sage, you must go back." His voice was so familiar. "You aren't safe."

He'd said her name! How was that possible? The woman nodded. "He's right. Leave us, dear. Be a good girl." Then she pulled something from her apron pocket. The pistol.

Sage shuddered and nausea rose in her throat.

Something touched her shoulder. She practically leapt into the air. The ghosts vanished. The cold dissipated.

"Are you all right?" Nate asked, his breath warm on her neck.

She could move now; she gripped her brother's arm. "Did you see that? Hear it? What just happened?"

"See what?" He took the phone still clutched in her hand. He waved the light about. "I don't see anything. Didn't hear anything either."

"I'm losing my mind, that's all. We're fine, we're all fine." She took back her phone. How had Jacob Huntley—because that's who the man had to be—known her name? And warned her to leave, as did Grandma Esther. The woman must be Grandma Esther. A lady in despair over unreturned love. But to kill? "We must find Patrick."

* * *

When Sage rounded the corner, she saw her cousin opening a door. A dim light filtered into the passage. A set of narrow stairs rose in front of them, similar to the ones she and Patrick had climbed when he broke into the house. But those had started on the second floor.

She stepped behind him, still jittery over the ghosts and their speaking to her. Was she special, with a connection to her family's past? This was the third time she'd 'seen' Grandma Esther. Should she tell the boys? Was she unsafe?

"It's like the Fun House at the amusement park." Patrick started to mount the stairs.

"You need to take this seriously. Don't be dense and careless." Sage's words came out rough, nearly angry.

Patrick turned and stared at her. Hurt flashed through his eyes, something she'd rarely seen during this visit. "I'm trying to distract myself, if it's anything to you."

Sage bristled at Patrick and his unfair situation. "Adults are going to do what they want. Just don't get anyone arrested or injured."

"Distract from what?" Nate asked, his hands on his hips. "No one tells me anything."

"His father is getting remarried." Sage said it calmly. "And we all have to deal with it. Right, Patrick?"

"Yeah, right. He's no longer my dad." Patrick frowned, then stomped up the stairs.

Sage knew she had to forgive her own dad for his fooling around. It would make things easier. Her shoulders sagged. At least he hadn't deserted them.

A murky light came from a tiny window high on the wall. She switched off her flashlight and followed her cousin, Nate on her heels. The ghostly conversation wouldn't leave her head. It seemed that her Grandma Esther *had* murdered her lover. Sage needed to boldly ask Huntley what he knew about the man who had to be his ancestor. No more being mysterious! She wished she were Christine's age, then people would take her seriously.

At the top of the stairs, they entered a long, shadowed hallway, cool and musty. Was this a fourth floor? The house was like a maze, inside a creepy funhouse, which wasn't much fun.

A window at the other end was stained glass. Faint colors filtered through it, leaving patterns on the floor. Patrick tried to open doors, but they were locked. Then he looked up.

He pointed. "A trapdoor. There's the attic."

"Why do you want to see the attic?" Nate asked. He sounded uneasy now. Sage wished he'd stayed home.

"Because that's where the really scary things are." Patrick glanced around. "We need a chair to reach it."

"What if the scary things don't show themselves to *you*?" She hadn't meant to sound boastful. If she told them what she'd seen and heard, would they laugh, or believe her? She could hardly believe it herself. Yet they had all witnessed the shifting shadow on the front porch.

"It will be gucci to find out what's up there." He didn't look amused, more like irritated. He jerked on another doorknob.

The ghost she thought of as Jacob had warned her to go back—she was in danger. And he knew her name. The extra scary part was, he'd sounded like Huntley, the current butler. She fought another tremble. Should she insist they leave?

A chill descended in the hall. It crept under her skin. The stained-glass patterns seemed to move, rearranging themselves to show colors on the wooden planks.

A door opened near her, and a child's pale face looked out. Bella! She crooked her finger at Sage.

Chapter 12

A haze settled around Sage, like she viewed the others through a filmy glass. She slipped to the side, eager to ask Bella a question. Was she real or another ghost? Why did these ghosts seek *her* out?

Bella's gaze and gesture drew her farther through the doorway. Sage felt like she floated as she followed her. Bella shut the door. Sage glanced down at the child, her reddish hair in its tight braids. She had a huge mud-stain on her apron. From drowning? Is that how she died? How could Sage even guess that's what happened?

"You dress from hundreds of years ago, but do you live here?" Sage asked.

"I exist. And used to visit. Right now, I must stay." Bella smiled, though her gaze remained serious. "Look at what I'm about to show you."

"Are you related to the Brubakers? I found a newspaper article." Sage persisted, her nerves tingling. "Are you a...ghost?"

"No one is who you might think they are. Behold." The little girl waved her arm and presented the room, like in a play.

When Sage gazed around her, she was stunned. Instead of a bedroom, she stood in a bright, beautiful living room filled with black and white box-shaped furniture. A bench had geometric designs.

"They call this Art Deco, whatever that means," Bella said.

Lively music came from an old phonograph. Sage had seen one in a museum. Light scents of perfume tickled her nose.

"They're having a party," Bella said. "They do that a lot."

People moved about near the front door and on the porch. Laughter tinkled from women, along with men's loud chuckles. The women wore sleek, narrow shifts, their hair cut short. The men in white suits and straw hats. *Am I in the 1920s, like in the old photos?*

Bella and Sage walked closer to the front door. No one seemed to notice them. Sage felt she only observed what was happening, as if really in a theater. The shock must be keeping her from collapsing.

The red-haired woman Sage had seen in the old pictures stood on the lawn.

"That's my great-great grandniece." Bella smiled, pointing. "I was never old enough to have my own children."

"Because...you died as a child," Sage found herself saying. Had she hit her head in one of Patrick's mischiefs and this was only a dream?

"Sadly, yes." Bella stared up at her with solemn eyes. "I was playing and, something happened, then I fell into the pond."

Sage rubbed her cheeks. How could this be real? "I'm so sorry."

A woman bustled past them. Sage gulped in a breath. She looked just like the vision she'd seen of her Grandma Esther. A pretty woman even with her dark hair pulled back in a bun.

Sage stared out at the people. The housekeeper—her two-greats grandmother—approached an elegant older woman on the lawn.

"That's Lawrence Brubaker's mother." Bella's eyes narrowed. "She's snooty but wants him to marry my descendant. Her husband, old John Brubaker, insists; he needs money. They're distant cousins. My family made money in the textile mills."

The mother, wearing a jeweled tiara, and long strings of pearls over a clinging mauve gown, lifted her pert chin high.

The red-haired woman, who wore an emerald-green dress with ruffled sleeves and a tie at the neck, sauntered over to them. Her green feathered headband wavered in the breeze, her feet encased in strapped, close-toed, green and silver shoes.

Grandma Esther nodded to the older lady and re-entered the house. "Grandma," Sage whispered.

"They can't see or hear us," Bella said.

"Why did you bring me here?" Sage asked the child, dread creeping over her.

"Isn't this what you're looking for, the secret of murder?"

How did the child know? Sage twinged then watched Grandma Esther walk through the living room in her black dress and long white apron.

A tall man in a loose, white suit entered the room. Another man followed him.

Sage pressed her hand against her clenching heart. The second man was the other ghost, the younger version of Huntley. He wore a maroon vest with gold buttons, just like Huntley.

"There is Lawrence." Bella nodded at the white-suited man. "He likes too many women, and spending money."

Lawrence laughed, his sharp-cheeked face still handsome despite a long jaw. He strode past them, out the front door.

The Huntley-like man turned to where her grandmother had gone.

Bella tugged on Sage's sleeve. "Let's follow him."

The two of them hurried, or rather floated after him like they were ghosts, and entered a hallway.

The housekeeper, Grandma Esther, was giving instructions to a young maid. She smiled when the man joined them. The maid scurried off.

"Jacob, when will we find time alone?" She held her hand up as if she ached to touch him. Then she patted down her hair under a white cap, her hazel eyes sparkling. "You've been avoiding me."

"Essie, I have something I need to tell you. But not here." Jacob backed off a step.

He looked about late twenties and definitely sounded British, where her grandmother must be in her late thirties. A doomed love affair.

"He's dumping her, that was the gossip," Sage whispered, anger rising over this long-ago event. But did she shoot him? So far the evidence seemed to hint that she did.

"Tragic but true." Bella shook her head, her braids swinging. "We're finished for now." The girl sounded so mature.

"How old are you, Bella?" Sage asked; her body felt odd, a slight swimming sensation.

"I'm ten. I'm big for my age." The child pulled Sage back to the living room.

"Could we stop my Grandma Esther from doing something terrible?" Sage didn't know if changing events in the past messed up the future.

"I've one more thing to tell you." The girl leaned close. "There's something horrible living in this house, in the attic mostly. It's greed and pride in a creature shape. But it goes out. Changes. Beware."

"You're joking, right?" The room swirled around Sage, faintness overtaking her. She felt like she was falling.

"Sage!" Nate's voice. He gripped her arm.

Sage blinked rapidly. She leaned against the wall in the gloomy upstairs hall, her knees weak.

Gazing around, it was like she had never moved. Yet her body felt limp and drained.

"You're acting weird." Her brother glared at her.

"Did I go...have I been here the whole time?" She rubbed her arms in the sudden chill. Had the scene with Bella been a dream? Could you smell perfume in a dream? She couldn't believe it. Had she gone Menty B? Having a mental breakdown?

"Of course you've been here. Where else would you be?" Nate groaned. "I'm trying to tell you Patrick found an open door."

Patrick dragged a chair across the floor and positioned it beneath the trapdoor.

Bella's words came back. Something horrible lived in the attic. She jumped forward and grabbed the chair. "Don't do this. I beg you."

Was the suppose occupant what they'd seen on the front porch that evening? Could it be what murdered their teacher? How could she trust any of this? It was like a crazy horror movie. But she was taking no chances.

"Let go. I'll just take a peek." Patrick jerked on the chair, eyes blazing.

"I hear someone coming," Sage lied as she held the wood firm, her knuckles white. Yet something was scratching overhead. "Let's get out of here. *Now*."

* * *

Jacob:

Sage, now I'll call her Sage, is the only one who hears it. That insidious creature. She must have the 'specialness' that could be useful. Or she might not be strong enough, or in too much danger for the outcome expected. And Bella, the stubborn child with the tragic ending, seems determined to show what happened that day involving Sage's Grandma Esther. (sigh) Essie, did I love her or use her? My family served the upper classes for centuries, in England and America, but I had to be the rogue, the womanizer.

My grandfather, a butler for a diplomat, was humiliated.

If Sage is the one, is the household ready for this? Am I? I shouldn't have gone upstairs the afternoon of the party. Some days the excruciating pain still echoes through me.

Chapter 13

Sage peeled potatoes in their kitchen, the peeler scraping off the brown skin in slow strokes, releasing a starchy scent. Her mom put a pot full of water to boil on the lit gas stove.

The dream, or whatever it was, with Bella, haunted Sage. Then the beast in the attic? Too horror-movie to be real. At least she'd gotten the boys out of the house before anyone noticed they weren't still in the library.

"Mom, did anyone in our family have...what do you call them...premonitions?"

"Seeing into the future? Like a fortune teller?" Jenny cut up the potatoes already peeled into quarters. She placed them in the pot.

"Or seeing into the past." Sage couldn't believe this 'talent' came out of nowhere. She scraped the rest of the skin off the potato and handed it to her mom.

"Well, my grandmother, don't laugh, liked to do seances with her friends. She swore she could really talk to the spirits." Jenny shrugged, her smile wry.

"Did you believe her?" Sage snatched another potato and began to peel it.

"When I was a child, I thought it thrilling." Jenny laughed. "But my mother was embarrassed."

"Who did Great-Grandma talk to, did she say?" Was there truth here, and this was where her talent came from? She wished she'd known Great-Grandmother Barbara.

"Why this interest?" Jenny rinsed off the potato, cut it into quarters, and put it into the pot. "Are you too involved in Lakeluster House? You should plan for high school, joining a track team, since you run all over the island."

"I'd enjoy an art team more. And I'm interested in our family history." And the manor's history, the various residents of the place. Sage slid her gaze to her mom. "What if Great-Great Grandma Esther really killed the other servant?"

"Many believed it to be true. But like I said, my mother refused to speak about it. She liked to pretend her life was lollipops and roses. That's how she got by. Grandma Barbara used to leave hints, as if she knew more than she'd admit, Esther being her mother. The big family scandal." Jenny pursed her mouth. "There's a diary my grandmother left behind. I haven't looked at it in years. Or barely looked at it. You might read that for information."

"Yes. Where is it?" Sage rippled with excitement. She quickly peeled this last potato, almost nicking her finger.

"Remember, they're her thoughts, and may not be exactly what happened. People slant the truth through their own eyes. There are some unpleasant entries, if I recall correctly." Jenny tapped her chin. "It's in a box in the storage room. I'll find it for you."

A half hour later, Sage opened the brown leather-covered diary. The paper smelled musty and mildewed. She settled on a chair in her bedroom, the deep-set window giving light through its wavy leaded pane.

She flipped through the pages where her great-grandmother wrote of her everyday life and events. Then the writing grew more intense.

They won't believe me. I'm an old fool, my family thinks. But my mother talks to me in my mind. Her voice so adamant. She has been gone fifteen years. She asks for forgiveness. Jacob tricked her, led her on. Broke her heart. "I gave mine to him," she said. What should she do to make amends?

Before his betrayal "we talked of so many things." He spoke of John Brubaker, who died swearing there was an evil force in the house. Two, or maybe more, of the Seven Deadly Sins. Was he teasing me?

Sage stopped reading; her breath sucked in. Didn't Bella mention the creature in the attic was Pride and Greed? She turned on her tablet and typed Seven

Deadly Sins. Yes, Greed and Pride were two of them.

This had to be a myth. It couldn't be true. But something deeper told her it was true. She swallowed slowly and read on.

The evil started with Harrison Brubaker, who built the house, Jacob insisted. This hotel magnate used and abused people. His first wife died young, a miserable woman. Harrison married her for money. She gave him no children. He didn't need her anymore. Rumors of poison.

My mother is so devastated, she keeps telling me. Jacob pursued a young maid. A pretty, silly, blonde fluff. "I couldn't let him hurt me like this! His sin is Lust!"

Did she shoot him? I'm afraid to know.

Sage felt the flush of heat on her face. Why couldn't certain men be faithful? Even her own father. Of course, women could be just as bad. But now Patrick's life was screwed up, his dad rarely seeing him, too busy with his new love.

Sage read on, scanning for clues.

"I hadn't meant to, my mind was overturned. Forgive me for this dreadful act," Mother pleads. "I first committed the sin of Lust, now it's Envy and Wrath."

Sage trembled. Grandma Esther must have killed Jacob, all the clues were there. And *she'd* inherited this strange power of talking to ghosts. A power that excited and scared her at the same time. These constant conflicting emotions were driving her crazy.

She scratched her scalp and continued to read.

"I hid it in a metal box, and buried it in the back garden, near the fountain," Mother says. *Hid what?*

The pistol?

Sage flipped through more pages, nothing about the box. Would it still be there? flashed through her mind. She sat up straighter, heart thumping. She needed to find out. And this time, she'd include the boys.

* * *

Dressed in dark clothing, like three burglars, or ninjas, Sage led her two assistants behind Lakeluster House, and around a crumbling stone wall. They all carried shovels. The shadows of dusk crept across the overgrown mess that had once been a garden. The July humidity had cooled a bit.

Dead plants, withered and scraggly weeds, both dried and fresh, tangled everywhere. In the middle sat a filthy fountain filled with brownish water and leaves. The stink of decay. The statue, which held a pot where the water must have once poured out, no longer had a head. A beheaded woman in a long robe.

Was this how Grandma Esther felt after...? Sage must be mental to even be here!

"Where do we start?" Nate asked, his expression earnest.

She stared at the house; the windows were blank, with no lights. "Close around the fountain, I guess. And be as quiet as possible."

"Our great-grandma actually 'spoke' to her dead mother? Creepy." Patrick snorted. He positioned his shovel and pushed with this foot. The earth was hard. He grunted and pushed with more force. "We don't even know if it was a pistol she buried. Do you even believe it was true she heard a voice?"

"I'm not sure of anything. This could be, what do the adults say, a wild goose chase? But I want to try." Sage started on the opposite side. This was nuts, but something compelled her to do it. She had the same curiosity as Patrick had in the beginning of their exploring the manor, but hoped she could keep hers under control. Yet, here they were, destroying property. She kept digging in the blade until she cracked the dried earth and dug up dark soil.

Worms wriggled in the moist dirt beneath. An earthy smell. She held her breath and kept going, her arms and shoulders aching. Nate was digging in front of the fountain. Forty minutes went by.

"We're wasting our time." Patrick stopped and leaned on his shovel. He'd dug up most of his side near the fountain. "I say we sneak in and open the trapdoor to the attic. Maybe the house can tell us more."

"We are making a horrible mess." Sage hid her disappointment, but she dug in again, loosening more soil. "And *no* trapdoor, Patrick. You could be in huge trouble." Was there really something up there? After her 'visit' with Bella, who knew what was possible?

She kept glancing at the house, expecting Huntley to throw open a window any moment and demand why they were there. Or the police had been called—was there a phone in the manor?—and soon they'd be in handcuffs.

The shadows lengthened. Nate was enjoying himself, hopping on the shovel to dig a deeper hole. A clink sounded. Nate blurted, "aha." He bent and clawed with his fingers. Sage and Patrick rushed over. She saw the top of a metal box.

They hunched down and cleared away the dirt. Patrick jerked on and pulled out the crusted metal box. With effort, he unlatched the rusted latch and opened the lid.

Wrapped in cloth, an old pistol lay inside. The three gushed out their breaths in unison.

A window creaked. Sage stared upwards.

The attic window was half open. Something stood there, an outline of darkness, watching them. A shout crawled up her throat.

Chapter 14

"We need to get out of here." Sage shut the lid. "Patrick, you carry the box."

Patrick frowned. "This is, *wow*, but I want to investigate—"

"I'm serious," she hissed. "Someone is watching us." She stood and brushed off the knees of her jeans.

"And I found the pistol. I'm a good investigator." Nate stood, his grin wide. Then he frowned. "Who's watching?"

Sage grabbed her brother's shoulder. "Get your shovel and hurry to the wall."

Patrick glared at the house as he stood with the box. "I don't see anyone."

"Well, I did." She refused to look up at the attic window again. Her skin prickled like ants swarmed over her. She snatched up her shovel. "Let's go."

"Who put you in charge?" Patrick asked. "I'm the older one."

Another window scraped open, this one on the first floor. Huntley peered out, his face stern. "What are you children doing? You're trespassing. You look like bloody grave robbers."

"I'll explain later." She gave him a quick smile over her alarm. "Please excuse us, Mr. Huntley."

Nate ran toward the wall. Patrick picked up his shovel, the box tight under his arm, and followed with a grumble.

Sage felt like she was ending a play. She almost bowed in her fluster, the shovel her sword. The butler her hostile audience. "Sorry, sir. We'll come back and clean it up. I promise."

Would he have them arrested? She had to visit tomorrow, or another day soon, to explain. If the cops didn't show up at her house first.

A glance to her right, she saw someone wearing a large straw hat dressed in a flowing gown, golden in the setting sun. The person was pulling weeds; a woman with blonde hair. She stared at Sage, then scurried away. How odd. How creepy!

Sage rushed after the boys. The three of them scrambled through the woods, branches whipping by. She wheezed over the jolt of her heart as the darkness draped around them.

* * *

The next morning, Nate scrolled through documents on his computer in his bedroom. "Fingerprints have been developed on items after forty years."

Sage leaned toward the screen. "But this would be a hundred years. Would our Grandma Esther's prints still be on the pistol?"

"We'd have to ask a…fingerprint history person." Patrick tapped the box next to him on Nate's bed. They'd cleaned the metal off the best they could, the pistol still nestled inside. "But that wouldn't prove she'd done the murder."

"Maybe Dad knows someone at the college?" Nate scrolled through more websites.

"We need a forensic expert." Sage had watched those CSI shows on TV. She fought a yawn after a restless night. The 'thing' she'd seen at the attic window haunted her dreams. It couldn't be real. Huntley playing tricks? Yet how could she explain her visions? And Bella, so real. Plus, who was the woman in the straw hat? Another ghost? Sage quivered, exhausted by it all. "I'll ask Dad. And don't touch that pistol, Patrick."

She still needed to visit Lakeluster House to calm down Huntley. Or were the police already on their way?

Downstairs, she found her father on the front porch sipping coffee, enjoying his Saturday. He looked over and smiled when he saw her.

"Sage. Good morning. Come sit with me." He patted the wicker chair beside him.

She did so, hands on her knees. The morning air was warm, with just a touch of humidity. She wished she felt more comfortable around him. Was the woman he'd had the affair with still living in Nahant? "Dad, I've been investigating the rumor that my Grandma Esther killed a man at Lakeluster House."

"Ah. We've all heard that speculation. That's quite a task for a young girl. Are you certain you want to do this?" He shifted to face her, brow furrowed. "How are you investigating? I hope you're being careful."

"I'm almost fourteen. I'm being careful." She wouldn't admit she wasn't that careful. "Anyway, I have a question." She stared off across the lawn for a moment. The sweet scent of her mom's roses drifted on the slight breeze. A bird twittered in the maple tree. "Do you know any forensic scientists?"

"You are serious. Why would you need a forensic scientist?" He fingered the rim of his cup, his gaze probing.

She stretched out her legs in her shorts. Legs that were too subby to her mind, though they had a decent shape. How she wished for long and graceful ones. "I had a crazy idea. I wonder how many years fingerprints lasted."

"A good question. I might be able to find out." He sipped his coffee. "Do you have a particular reason for wanting to know this?"

She couldn't tell him about the pistol, or them digging up a garden. Her parents would ground her until her eighteenth birthday. "I was only curious."

"Are you too caught up in this, after these many visits out to the manor?" He'd put on his no-nonsense fatherly voice. "Your mother is concerned. And so am I."

"There's nothing to worry about." She tried not to sound defensive. But there was plenty to worry about. "Just, if you could find out, that would be great." Or it was just another wild goose chase. Patrick was right; what would it prove? Anyone could have handled the pistol. Or was it an excuse to talk to her father? She missed their closeness.

"All right. I'll inquire, dear. But I wish you'd find other interests." Minutes of silence ticked by. She pushed on the chair arms. He cleared his throat. "I heard about Patrick's father, marrying his young girlfriend."

Sage stiffened. "Patrick is really upset."

He placed a hand on her shoulder. "We've never discussed what happened between me and your mother two years ago. You were young then. But like you said, you're almost fourteen."

She drew her feet under the chair again, ready to stand. "We don't have—"

"We need to clear the air. I made a terrible mistake and hurt your mom. And you kids. I'm sorry about that. I want you to understand, people sometimes do foolish things." He squeezed her shoulder. "I was wrong."

Her throat thickened. Could it be wiped away so easily? "Do you still love Mom?"

"I never stopped loving your mother." He sighed. "I was selfish."

Then why did you do it? She bit back that question. He wanted forgiveness, and she wasn't certain she was ready to give it. Though it would make things easier between them.

"Okay. We'll talk about this again when I'm sixteen." She stood, her words almost teasing, a mask for her discomfort. She felt a step closer to him, but at the same time wanted to leave.

He stared up, his dark brown eyes sad. His thick black hair framed his handsome face. "I love all of you. And I'll ask at the college about contacting any forensic experts. But fingerprints would have to be in a database to be traceable. Would this person have been fingerprinted in the first place?"

"I never thought of that." She drooped and saw the waste of this idea. And Grandma Esther obviously 'touched' the pistol to even hide it in the metal box. "I guess we can forget it. Thanks for offering."

"You can ask me anything, you do know that? People get caught up in...it's no excuse. Patrick's dad is wrong to desert his family. But maybe your Aunt Theresa will find someone better, less boastful." Dad sighed and squeezed her hand. "It's still painful for the boy. But I hope you forgive me."

"Yeah, I will. I do." She meant it, since it was the grown-up thing to do. Sage smiled as best she could and left the porch.

Relationships were so complicated, past and present. But now she had to hurry out to the manor before the sheriff pulled up, lights flashing.

* * *

Huntley stood, hands on his hips, while Sage filled in the holes they'd dug the previous evening. "You're fortunate I didn't bring in the police. This was terrible mischief. What were you looking for?"

"You won't believe me if I tell you." She patted down the earth with her shovel, his presence unsettling. Then she moved to the next hole. "You're right. We shouldn't have done this."

"Did you read about buried treasure? A child's fantasy? Or some such rot." His gaze jabbed into her.

"You should fix up this garden. Plant new plants." Sage gave a quick glance at the attic window. What had she really seen up there?

Huntley walked closer. "Answer my question, Miss Emery. What were you looking for?"

His menacing tone sent tremors along her shoulders.

"A pistol." She shoved dirt into the next hole. How much should she admit?

"How did you know where to look?" His voice had softened, but it remained intimidating.

"A diary left by one of my relatives." Her words clipped out. She met his glare.

His face had blanched white, his eyes blue slits. "Are you getting closer to the truth?"

Sage swallowed hard. She wanted him on her side. How else would she have access to the house? "I'm sorry we destroyed the yard. We should have asked permission."

He folded his arms over his maroon vest. "But would you have received it? I've already allowed you to use the library, poking around where you shouldn't."

"That's what confuses me." She gripped the shovel handle to steady herself. "You don't even ask if we found the pistol, I mean who wrote the diary."

He cocked his head, eyes sparking. "I think you meant pistol."

She blew out her breath. "Okay. You don't ask if we found it. Or what the gun was for. As if you already know."

"I can't let matters come to light too easily, now can I?" He smiled, though his gaze stayed hard.

Were they playing a game? A dangerous game that could hurt her. "It was your ancestor who was murdered, wasn't it?"

"Perhaps." His reply held so many secrets; his left eyebrow arched. "Things aren't always what they seem. And some truths should stay buried."

Sage should run, but again, the mystery tugged at her, a connection to this place that baffled her. Jacob's ghost had known her name and warned her in the secret passage. How was that possible? Was Huntley also aware of the spirits? Did they have a connection? He concealed far too much.

The rear door opened. Miss Dora stood there, her smile sweet. "Won't you come in, Miss Emery?"

Sage froze in place. How much information could she get from her?

Chapter 15

The teacup before her on the table in the small parlor off the kitchen, Sage smiled at Miss Dora. She hoped she looked calm after her frantic hole-filling in the garden. "Thank you for inviting me in."

Miss Dora wore thick glasses today, her gaze clear, which was somehow unnerving. As if now she could really see what was going on. "Were you helping to clean up my garden, Miss Emery?"

Huntley stood close by. He gave a slight nod. "She was, indeed, my lady."

"In England we had a lovely garden." Miss Dora sighed. "This one was lovely, too, when I was a child."

"You came here as a child?" Sage sipped her tea, more milk and sugar than brew, hiding her surprise.

"Oh, yes. I was born here. But my mother and father had a disagreement, and she took me to live in England." A sadness passed over her round face. "I was practically a baby."

"I understand about disagreements." Sage thought of her talk with her father that morning.

She glanced at the green lions on the sideboard; their eyes remained blank, thank goodness.

"When I was about ten, we came for a visit." Miss Dora gazed around the room, her smile bright. "What a grand house this seemed to me then."

Sage had heard the manor was deserted for many years and it certainly was neglected. A musty smell still clung to everything.

"Why did you decide to come back?" Sage kept glancing at the woman's head, her hair. Would there be blood? No, no, too ridiculous.

"Oh, there were old issues to clear up." Miss Dora sipped her tea.

"Did you find any interesting..." How to ask. Sage glanced at Huntley. "People, or maybe signs of ghosts, here?" There, she'd said it. She'd tried to make it sound like an adventure.

Huntley straightened, his gaze probing.

"Well, I did meet a little girl playing on the stairs. She had long, red braids. She told me she knew Harrison Brubaker, my long-ago ancestor." Miss Dora laughed. She fingered the lace collar on her plain blue dress. "But I didn't believe her. She seemed a strange child."

Bella! Sage squirmed in the chair. "What else did she say?"

"She said she saw him do something bad." Miss Dora leaned close. "And then she vanished."

Was Bella from the time of Harrison Brubaker? She could have been from the dates she'd read in the old newspaper article. "You never saw her again?"

"Sadly no, and we went back to England shortly after." She slid her teacup toward the butler. He lifted the pot and poured her a fresh cup. "We visited again a couple of years later. Then no more."

"Have you seen anyone else since you moved back in? Old houses are full of mysterious things." Sage pressed on, despite Huntley's continued stare on her.

"I do remember, when I was a child, a cat scratching in the attic. It sounded huge. I wanted to rescue it, but my father said no." The woman pouted like a child as she stirred sugar into her tea.

The scratching. Sage chilled. The creature. How weird her life had become. She trembled and sipped more tea. And, Huntley, he seemed aware of all of this. He acted like he wanted her to find out more, then he'd hold back. What was his game?

"Have you learned more about your ancestor, the one who worked here? There was a murder, I think." Miss Dora tilted her gray-curled head. A gash of red appeared on her left cheek, but quickly vanished.

Sage felt a jab of cold in her stomach. How could she deny she'd seen these things? What did it mean?

"Though I hate to speak of such incidents, wasn't a man shot?" Miss Dora asked.

Huntley moved away from the wall, frowning, his hand pressed to his chest, as if he suffered a pain. An expression of misery briefly changed his face.

Sage pictured the ghost of Jacob, the same acute blue eyes as the butler. A shocking idea ripped through her. But it *couldn't* be! She needed to leave. To unpack all the information and the suspicions storming through her brain.

"I haven't learned much more." *Except, I believe my two-greats grandmother murdered her lover.* She stood. "Excuse me, but my mom expects me home. I hope I can come again. Thank you for the tea."

Was Huntley 'feeling' what his ancestor felt, or was it something scarier?

She turned and stalked through the house toward the front door, her breath rasping in her throat.

* * *

Lilah shifted on the rock, her hair swept up by the wind. "I'm beginning to wonder if you're dreaming most of this. Or more like having nightmares."

Sage stared along the rocky shoreline, the waves crashing, her hand rubbing on the rough stone she perched on. They sat on the edge of Lodge Park, a green expanse on the tip of Nahant. Broad Sound met the Atlantic in a swirl of turquoise water around the craggy finger that hooked out from Nahant's southeastern shore.

"It does sound cray—cray. And now I suspect the butler is the same 'person' as Jacob." That thought jumped into her head while watching Huntley's reaction. "But it's not possible."

"The same one your Grandma Esther shot a hundred years ago? Her great love." Lilah twisted her hair to hold it down, her gaze concerned. "No, that's absurd."

Huntley was so real, a solid presence, yet he held too many secrets. Why did he warn and allow her access at the same time? Anything *seemed* possible in this new realm she explored. Like a fairy-tale gone bad.

"But the rest of it. Bella, and the others. I swear they came to me. Even Miss Dora mentioned Bella." Sage brushed her hair from her face. The wind whistled through the twisted rocks below. Miss Dora confirmed Sage wasn't totally imagining things. Or they were both losing their minds. If the odd Miss Dora hadn't already. And what of those bloody-looking gashes on her head? The blood on her fingers.

"You said your great-grandmother wrote in her diary that her mom spoke to her, in her mind?" Lilah asked, her voice edged with doubt. She crossed her legs, slim in light lilac pants.

"Our whole family is nuts, in one way or another." Sage forced a laugh. "But it could be a rare talent."

Should she embrace it or run in the other direction?

"If Mr. Saunders hadn't been found killed, I wouldn't believe much of it." Lilah shrugged, then winked. "Or I'd have a hard time. But I know you're not a liar."

"I don't blame you for doubts." Sage had yet to speak of the 'thing' supposedly in the attic. Lilah *would* think her insane. Was she losing the support of her best friend with these wild tales? The manor had crept under her skin, and she couldn't push it out.

Seabirds cawed, floating on the wind. The loamy smell of grass and the salty sea refreshed Sage, washing away or rearranging the cobwebs of her worries. She tapped the heels of her slip-on pink sneakers against the rock. Sneakers that matched her pink shorts.

"Girl, you need a break from the ghouls. I've been practicing songs from *Grease*. For the high school tryout." Lilah took a deep breath. She started to sing "Summer Nights."

"Your voice is good. But you need the boys' side to make sense." Sage laughed, and it felt a relief. A knot untying.

"You play the boys. Do you remember their crass words? I can hardly practice at home with four pains-in-the-butt brothers and sisters. My dad doesn't even want me to do musicals or acting." Lilah slowly braided her hair, the blonde strands shining in the sunlight. "He'll probably want me to go to the naval academy like he did."

"My parents want me to have other interests." Sage needed to prepare for the big shift in her life—high school on the mainland. Kids she hadn't yet met. At least Lilah would be with her. She tossed a pebble down the cliffside. "I might try out for Drama too, along with insisting I do everyone's make-up. I'm asking my mom for a professional kit to create facial designs. That should please her; nothing to do with ghosts."

"Good. I..." Lilah turned.

A family with two loud little boys were roaming through the park not far off. The boys chased one another, squealing, then the family wandered farther up the coast where WWII bunkers had been built, though no one could access them.

"Tourist interruption." Sage sighed. "With no sandy beaches at this end, it's usually quieter."

"My sister, the *big* seventeen, went to the fourth of July celebration in town," Lilah said. "She says a group of young tourist guys got drunk and punched each other out. Mom wouldn't let me go." She made an exaggerated sad face, her wrist against her forehead.

"I know, we're still children to them." Sage groaned, caught between childhood and deeper into teenage-hood, an uncomfortable place. Yet lately, she felt more adult than ever. She might not have long slender legs, but her growing breasts pushed against her blouse—almost an embarrassment. "My cousin Patrick wanted to go; he wasn't happy when Mom said no."

"When is he happy these days? Sucks about his dad remarrying. Hey, you need to ask this Huntley about our teacher. Who could have done such a horrible thing to him? See what the butler says. From what you've told me, he seems to like you. Or tolerate you. He was there at the manor when it happened." Lilah belted out another line from "Summer Nights."

The butler did it, a cliché Sage had heard. Did Huntley like her, or was he drawing her into a dangerous place to silence her? She hunched her shoulders to contain her burst of nerves. "Mr. Saunders's daughter said her father spoke with a man he called J. H. It *has* to be Huntley. I'll ask and won't be pushed off."

It had been talked about at the first tea party, but Huntley was vague about anyone asking about the manor's history. And what had Bella seen—Miss Dora's words—that was bad? Despite the warm air, Sage's arms goose-bumped.

Chapter 16

The following day, Sage stood once more in the manor library. She faced Huntley, hesitant but determined. "I have lots of questions for you. But first, we found a secret passage. Did you know about it? My cousin pressed here, and the side panel opened up." She ran her finger around the crest carved on the fireplace mantel—though she didn't dare press too hard.

"Did you, indeed? I shouldn't have left you overly snooping children alone." Huntley smirked, his eyes like blue flint. He walked over and pushed on the crest. Nothing happened.

Sage widened her eyes. How could this be? Another trick?

Huntley moved back and stood near a rusted candelabra of lit candles—to chase the gloom from this overcast day. His high forehead gleamed under light brown hair. One lock fell forward. Did he look younger today? "What are your questions? What do you hope to discover, Miss Emery?"

Sage pressed hard on the crest; nothing. Had she dreamed it? No, it was real. Then she swore one of the lions winked at her. She jerked her hand away. "Uh...clues about my Grandma Esther, who worked as a housekeeper when John Brubaker owned the property." She tried to sound businesslike. "His son Lawrence soon took over."

"I am quite aware of the family history." Huntley grimaced, yet sadness clouded his eyes.

Her suspicion increased. "Sometimes I wonder if you didn't live through the history." She watched a flicker in his gaze. Would he throw her out for being rude? *Could* she trust him?

"Or died...?" He smiled, though it looked grim. He was taunting her. "How much do you understand about what happened?"

A chill traveled up her back. "Help me understand. Are you a ghost?" She said it as a joke, sort of, but walked farther away from him, toward the back bookcase.

"An interesting assumption. Quite peculiar. Define ghost, Miss Emery." He tapped his fingers on his crossed arms. Today he wore a navy-blue vest with similar gold buttons, though it looked threadbare in places.

Her frustration rose at his smug words. He didn't waver or look transparent like the ghosts she'd seen. But then, neither did Bella. "You seemed in pain when Miss Dora mentioned the shooting; the murder."

"A slip of the moment. Can I not feel empathy for a young man who was killed?" Now his eyes narrowed. Had she gone too far? Or did he dismiss her as a child who could cause little harm? He seemed to enjoy the challenge of their conversation. As did she—even with a slice of caution.

She fingered the smooth leather spines of the books. It was better to change the subject. "I want to talk about my history teacher, Mr. Saunders. He left notes. One said he spoke with a man with the initials J. H."

Huntley nodded slowly. "I did speak to this meddling interloper. He asked too many questions." He finally admitted it. "What else was in these notes?"

"I don't know." Her pulse quickened. Was interloper the same as trespasser? "He was found murdered a month after you moved in. Were you questioned by the police?"

"Of course. But I knew nothing. And I told Miss Dora nothing. She is delicate and...likes to be protected." He arched an eyebrow—his go-to expression.

"How could she not know when it happened so close?" Sage fisted her hands to calm her racing thoughts. Miss Dora liked living under a rock, like her Grandma Jean. "Who would kill him like that? Skinned, it was said."

"That does sound repulsive. I'll let you in on a secret." He stepped close to her, towering over her. "I've never killed anyone."

"I'm glad, but Mr. Saunders was a wonderful teacher. Do you know who did it?" The *thing* in the attic? Sage resisted sliding away—she felt no real menace from him today. Or was she being stupid? She inhaled through a tight throat and struggled not to show fear.

"It probably wouldn't do you any good to know. And maybe this would be beyond your comprehension." He moved back, his expression stern. "Perhaps you should forget it for your own safety."

"But I can't. I see ghosts. They talk to me." She blurted this out, then covered her mouth for a second. "Only since I've come to this manor." Sage almost described the deadly sins Bella said the creature was formed from. All this craziness had become her normal.

"Jacob has talked to you. Didn't he warn you?" Huntley's words were low and even.

Her knees weak, she longed for a chair. *Are you and Jacob the same person?* "How do you know that?"

He smiled again, eyes glinting. "Maybe I, too, speak to ghosts."

Didn't she have her answers? Her Grandma Esther *must* have killed her lover. And the monster in the attic probably murdered Mr. Saunders. But weren't monsters only things of horror movies and nightmares? Her head throbbed.

Huntley cupped her elbow. "You look very pale. We've enjoyed your company, but perhaps your exploration of Lakeluster is over." He said it with a tinge of disappointment at her lack of courage.

He led her to the desk, pulled out the chair, and helped her sit. "You should rest before you go."

She pressed her hands on her thighs. She would get her courage back. "One more question. What hides in the attic?"

Huntley sighed and stared at the ceiling. "You're a clever girl. But there are things neither of us could feasibly understand, my dear. Nor should we try. Now you ask too many questions."

He didn't deny it! She half-wished he would. Did she intend to wrestle with that much danger? Would she end up hanging by the lake? She touched her throat and wondered if she should bow out from this insane situation.

She met his gaze again. "You've let me ask or poke around; but why was Mr. Saunders—?"

"I've protected you." He stared down, brow furrowed. "But you can only stir up so much until matters...increase. Do you have the gumption?"

A word she'd have to look up to make certain of its meaning. But she was sure she had some. She felt a part of the manor, attached in many strange ways. Her stubbornness made her brave. *Yes, I like the*

surging in my veins, exciting every nerve!
She needed to speak to Bella again.

* * *

"We need to hide that pistol," Sage said after she called the boys into her bedroom once she'd returned from Lakeluster House. Her dismissal from Huntley didn't sound final, or she only wished it to be so. Had he confirmed that something lurked in the attic with no outright denial? She rubbed under her chin; so many unknowns.

Her bedroom, once fluffy pink with unicorns, was now darker. She'd filled it with posters of women in lavish make-up, cat's eyes, shiny lips, actors made up as zombies and other creatures; the art Sage intended to master.

"Why? Don't you want to prove our Grandma Esther used it to kill her love?" Patrick sat cross-legged on the floor, his gaze stubborn. The metal box was beside him. Nate sat on his other side.

"All we'd prove is it's the same type of gun. Is that written down somewhere?" Sage sat on her bed. "Grandma Esther wouldn't have been fingerprinted, so that's another dead end."

"There were no databases for prints back then," Nate put in. "I thought of that later. Should we tell our parents we have the gun?"

136

Recently, her brother liked to read detective novels and scan the internet for unsolved murders. He wanted it to make him braver, but often told Sage it wasn't easy.

"No, we'd be banned from the manor." Or would that be a good thing? She'd already told her dad too much. He would be suspicious.

"You're right. We'd better put it in our attic." Nate shrugged. "I looked it up. It's a Browning from 1922."

"I hate to hide it away. I want to see if the pistol still fires." Patrick started to unlatch the metal box.

Sage leaned down and pressed on the lid. "Don't touch it. If it's loaded, you could hurt yourself."

"You're not my boss, bro." Patrick grumbled. He swiped a hunk of blond hair from his eye. He needed a haircut. "I started this adventure. And now you're at the manor more than anyone. Stop sneaking out there. What did you learn?"

Sage stared at the zombie poster, then back at them. "If I told you the truth, you'd laugh at me. And I'm not your brother, bro."

"What's the truth? Tell us." Nate grinned up at her and winked, though his gaze showed concern.

She was torn by this truth. "We might be done. Mystery solved. Grandma Esther killed the servant, Jacob." She pictured Huntley again—was it impossible?

"How can you be sure?" Patrick sneered. "And who murdered Mr. Saunders?"

"If I could trust you not to go off so high key, breaking into the house, trying trapdoors, I might tell you." Sage stiffened her shoulders. "What if I said ghosts talked to me? That's how I know some of what happened."

Patrick laughed and slapped his knee. "Sounds like fun, but you've got to be lying."

"Weren't you the one who said there were skeletons and other spooky things in the house?" Sage remembered their first visit, or spying, this summer.

"What about the scary person we saw on the front porch?" Nate asked in earnest.

"That's the part I still don't understand all the details." She understood only pieces of this madness; what was true, and what wasn't? "The person looked like a shapeshifter." The creature Bella insisted lived in the attic? Sage bunched her bed quilt in her fingers.

"Do you really talk to ghosts?" Nate's dark eyes looked skeptical.

"Are shapeshifters real? But it did look creepy. The next time you go, I'm going with you." Patrick hopped to his feet. "You can show me these ghosts. Have your *discussions*." He obviously didn't believe her.

Patrick picked up the box. Sage stood and grabbed it from him. The gun rattled inside. He huffed and scowled.

"You have to be careful. I'm warning you." She gripped the box and wasn't sure Huntley would allow them back in. Was the butler done with her? She felt a strange sadness. "I don't want my brother hurt."

Nate stood, rolling his eyes. "I'm not a baby, Sage. I'm almost twelve."

Sage wanted to return, to speak to Bella, if she could. She had to convince Huntley to welcome her back into the manor. How to slip away from the boys? Or should she take them for security? She fought a groan. Only if she could keep Patrick from running wild.

Huntley said he'd protected her. But how could she glimpse a monster—if such a thing existed—and not risk putting all their lives in danger?

Chapter 17

Nate kicked his legs, sending the rope swing higher. It creaked against the huge branch of the spreading oak tree that overlooked the pond. The wooden seat looked splintered and hopefully wouldn't crack.

Sage watched him then glanced at the quiet manor behind her, and back again. A group of scoters, a duck with a large brown head, flapped and foraged in the pond on the far side. Mid-morning, the humidity had yet to thicken the air. The pond smelled dank. Mossy plants clung to its shore.

Patrick nudged her. "Is that where your teacher was found, mutilated and hanging from that branch?"

Sage cringed. "The branch next to it, according to rumors. And I warned you about poking me."

"Maybe blood splashed on the rope swing." Patrick made a Dracula-toned voice. "*Boohaha.* What animal or person could do such a gross thing?"

"That's what I'd like to know." A scratching in the attic? Should Sage try to peek up there? Her curiosity was deep—too deep. She leaned over and glanced at her reflection in the pond. In the murky water something white floated by; material, an apron? Then the fabric was gone. She stepped back and bumped into her cousin.

"What's wrong with you? Why don't we just go over and knock?" Patrick picked up a stick and flung it into the water. The ducks quacked in irritation.

"I already told you. I'm not sure we'd be welcome inside." Two days ago, in the library, Huntley had said her exploring was over. This way, their activity might draw someone out. She needed to stay connected. Was it her Grandma Esther or something else that pulled at her? "Nate, make some loud happy noises."

"Yippi! I'm so happy!" Nate called, head back; legs straight out, he swung the swing forward. One duck flew off.

"Did you piss off the butler?" Patrick laughed. "Our perfect Sage—"

"Don't laugh. I'm not perfect. You *have* to act grown up." She pinned him with her gaze. "If you would, I might tell you more. This is serious. We need to be a team."

"Okay. But how can you really talk to ghosts? Ask them to talk to me to prove it." Patrick smirked. He shifted his feet in scuffed sneakers.

Sage looked him over in his red striped tee shirt and straight-leg jeans—this boy who had changed so much in the three years since his last visit. "What other stuff do you like besides football?"

"Umm. I like baseball. I also like girls. Your girlfriend Lilah is really cute." Patrick's cheeks flushed. "All that blonde hair."

"She's too young to date, so stay away," Sage said. "Her dad would chase you off with an anchor."

"I'll stay away, stupid." He hunched his shoulders. "I've decided I'm going be strong and take care of my mom, since my dad will ignore us."

"Maybe he won't." Sage hoped he wouldn't. How could a father just walk away from his children?

"Happy, happy, happy!" Nate called. The swing swished by, its ropes scraping the branch bark. Two more ducks flapped and flew away.

The front door opened. Huntley strode out, his steely eyes on them.

"What have I said about trespassing?" He didn't sound angry, only annoyed at what to do with such pests.

Sage smiled her widest and walked toward the porch. "Aren't you lonely out here without our company, sir?"

He leaned against the porch post, his smile quick. "Amusing. You are a stubborn young lady. What is it you want now?"

Sage sucked in her breath, ready to be bold. "I've talked to a girl named Bella. I'd like to visit her again."

Huntley cocked his head as if thinking it over. "This has turned into a dangerous folly, my dear. For your own safety—"

"But we're courageous!" Patrick ran up beside her. "And...I'll behave. I think."

"You'd better," Sage whispered to him, then she looked at the butler. "Could we visit the third floor? I saw Bella there one time before."

Huntley straightened, his gaze uneasy, but this time he didn't deny she existed. "I have my doubts about this venture. I may have permitted too much access. However, if I allow it, I'll have to come with you."

"And the attic—oww!" Patrick rubbed his upper arm where Sage pinched him.

"You promised," she said as evenly as possible. "Act grown up. You brag you're the oldest."

Nate joined them, puffing, his face rosy with exertion. "Are we going to be let in?"

"The kind Mr. Huntley offered to take us to the third floor." Sage sounded sickly sweet, something she didn't enjoy.

Huntley scowled at Patrick. "I agree, young man; you need to act more mature and not so impulsive. That behavior might take you dark places you don't care to be."

"Okay. I'll try real hard." Patrick scuffed his toe in the dirt. "Not a problem."

"My sister says she speaks to ghosts," Nate said brightly.

"Nate, we don't need to talk about that." Sage bristled with Huntley's comment to

Patrick. *Dark places you don't care to be.* Was she pushing too hard? She sought the thrill, but as usual wished her brother had stayed home.

Huntley stepped to the door and opened it. He lowered his eyebrows, looking very severe; his voice deepened. "Then come along, you three encroachers. Enter at your own risk."

"You sound like a bad movie, sir." Sage laughed, but it was brittle. Her nerves bunched, she and the boys walked into the manor.

* * *

On the third floor, Sage stared at the door where Bella had gestured to her previously. Their strange trip into the 1920s. She also looked for the giant scratch, but it was gone. She had to face it; these things *were* happening to her. Her connection to the past was real. Totally outrageous, but somehow real. She filled with the unsettling idea she had some sort of magic inside her.

"Any ghosts?" Nate watched her as if waiting for her to speak to something he couldn't see.

"Not yet." She took in a hallway that looked narrower with darker shadows. The stained-glass window at the end had rearranged its colors again. The musty smell thickened. "Don't wander off."

Patrick tried the locked doors. "Can't you open any of these?"

"Only certain people can, when it's required." Huntley stood against the wall, his arms crossed. His favorite pose. "You shouldn't be so impatient, young man."

"What is up in the attic?" Patrick asked, gaping at the trapdoor. He glanced at Sage. "I'm only wondering."

"Oh, just a few deadly sins, evolved over time," Huntley said, his voice dry. "What else do you hope to find up here?"

Sage cringed, remembering Bella's words about Greed and Pride. Was murder a deadly sin? She would think so.

"*Is* there anything in the attic?" She decided to be blunt again. She was as curious as Patrick but pretended calmness.

"Junk, rats, perhaps a malevolent spirit." Huntley gave a wry smile, though it seemed forced. "Don't all haunted houses have such things?"

She wasn't sure what malevolent meant, but it couldn't be good. "Can you show us the spirit?" she taunted him back.

"Now you're talking." Patrick's eyes gleamed with excitement. He clapped his hands. "Show me the evidence. Is it a walking skeleton?"

"Scary. But not real, right?" Nate sounded unsure and Sage regretted again that he was with them.

"It's not a wise idea." Huntley's penetrating gaze swept over them all. "You might make it angry, and we wouldn't want that." His eyes locked on Sage. "I can only offer so much protection. We've had our fun. Now we should go. Perhaps Bella can't come today."

"Did Mr. Saunders make it angry?" Sage asked, her face heating with frustration. She listened for any scratching noises from above. Why did she keep persisting? It's like the butler dangled bait before her, then pulled it back. Was he testing her? How could she trust him? Yet he seemed, when he wished, to nudge her toward the clues.

"What do you know about a spirit in the attic?" Patrick turned an accusing glare on her. "What's up there? Who told you about it? And who is Bella?"

Perhaps being connected to this family will not keep you safe.

Sage gulped. Huntley had said this, she heard it, but it was more in both their heads than real conversation. What did he mean by connection to the family?

"Yeah, who is Bella?" Nate asked.

About to defend herself, a chill rippled through Sage. A wavy feeling swirled inside her. The people before her faded, their voices distant. A hand touched her back. She whirled around.

Bella hovered there, her brow furrowed. She had more mud on her apron over her long, drab dress. "I'm glad you came. Are you ready to see what happened?"

Sage could only nod. Somehow, she knew what the child meant. Bella opened a door and pointed. Sage entered on nearly floating feet. Her heart thundered.

Grandma Esther stood in a small bedroom, her brunette hair loose and tumbled over her shoulders, making her look younger. The room was plain, with a narrow bed and gloom in the corners. She smiled sadly. "I wish this had never taken place. I was distraught. Betrayed. Don't ever fall for a man's honeyed words."

Sage tried to speak but couldn't. Her throat felt dry, tight.

Huntley was suddenly at the doorway. "Miss Emery, come back into the hall."

Sage nearly shouted, *no*! He'd followed her into the past—or was it his past, too?

Grandma Esther raised her chin. She pulled a pistol from her apron pocket. "You think you could dismiss me so easily, Jacob?"

Huntley started, then went to her, arms wide in obvious upset. "It has to be this way, Essie. We were only a fling."

Don't do it! Sage cried the words, but they stayed in her head and never left her mouth. She couldn't move her feet. She ached to save both of them.

"You can't change anything," Bella whispered as she fingered one braid.

"I loved you. And you chose that young, blonde floozy." Grandma Esther lifted the pistol, holding it with both hands.

Huntley reached out, as if to grab the gun. "Calm down, Es. Let's talk. Why do you keep returning here? All these decades. It's long over."

"I thought we had a future. Barbara needs a father. I see now you could never be that man. You lied to me to get what you wanted." Grandma Esther pulled the trigger. A shot blasted. She lurched back. Huntley gasped and clutched his chest. Blood seeped from a wound, scarlet and spreading.

The blast of noise ricocheted through Sage's brain, and she screamed.

Chapter 18

Rubbing her eyes, Sage was back in the hall, but Patrick and Nate weren't there. More chills quivered through her, her throat raw from the scream. She leaned against the wall and shuddered. "Is that what happened? I'm so confused about how to understand—I mean how I'm able to be a part of it. But where are the boys? Where did they go?" Panic surged inside her, hurting her chest.

Bella touched her arm. "Don't worry, they are exactly where you left them. This is a different dimension."

"How can any of this be? I did suspect it, though. Huntley *is* a ghost, and my Grandma Esther killed him. A hundred years ago." Sage pulled herself together with a tightening of her muscles and studied the girl before her. "And you're from many years before that."

"I am. I wander this house, trying to find a way out." Bella smiled sadly, her gaze mournful.

Sage struggled to order her thoughts.

"What happened to you? Did you see something you shouldn't have?" Sage glanced in every corner for the boys among the shadows. How did other dimensions work?

"Harrison Brubaker was tired of his wife. She hated it here. She gave him no children." Bella spoke with quiet sorrow. "I was the daughter of his cousin. I saw him put something in her tea. He persuaded her to drink it." She wrinkled her nose. "Then she got sick and died."

"And he knew you'd seen what he'd done?" Sage trembled with the cold and fear for a girl already beyond danger.

"He must have. I was afraid to tell anyone. My siblings were older; they'd laugh at me. But when I played near the pond, Mr. Brubaker threatened me, then pushed me in. I couldn't swim." The child spread out her soiled apron. "The pond mud clings to me."

"That's terrible." Sage's heart grew heavy with pity for Bella—a murdered child. She wanted to hug her. "I'm so sorry."

Bella stared at the trapdoor. "That's when it started. The Greed and Pride, then Wrath, piecing together in a horrible beast." The child whispered, "you could help us."

"Me? How could I help? That beast must have killed my teacher." Sage still hated to believe such a creature existed. And what sin had Mr. Saunders encouraged? She needed to see it, but the idea terrified her. Her brain buzzed as if it swarmed with bees. Was Huntley still lying dead in the bedroom? But how could a ghost lie dead?

A hand clasped her shoulder. She jumped. Bella stepped back and dissolved into the opposite wall.

Sage turned. Huntley stood behind her. He had no blood on his clothing.

"You are the Jacob I've seen with my Grandma Esther. You're the same person." She tried to steady her breathing. "All this time, you were a ghost."

"You've discovered the truth at last, Miss Emery." He smiled sadly. "At first, I wasn't sure I should allow you to decipher the details. It could be dangerous. But you were insistent and intelligent. It was an interesting experiment. And Bella persisted in showing you the past. She wants freedom, it's obvious." He shrugged. "I regret my behavior toward Esther. She had a bad marriage and her husband left her little money. However, I was a cad."

She agreed, if 'cad' was what she thought it was, but said nothing. Still, he didn't deserve to die. Disappointment that he wasn't flesh and blood overwhelmed her. She fisted her hands. "I'm sorry Grandma Esther shot you. Are you all stuck here, because of..." She stared up at the trapdoor. This time, she heard the scratching. She didn't say, 'because of your own sins.' "What about all those years the house was empty?"

"Was it really empty, my dear?" His eyes glistened. He looked so solid, so real. She resisted touching him. "Or were we waiting to be discovered again?"

By me? Her heart thudded. "What about Miss Dora? Is she a ghost, too?"

Nate, out of nowhere, barged up to her and grabbed her arm. "Did you talk to who you wanted? Did you find out any more about our Grandma Esther?"

Sage almost hugged him, but he'd object. "A little. Not enough." Had the dimensions clashed together? She staggered under the weight of it. "Where's Patrick?"

"I'm here. What are you keeping from us? Stop throwing shade." He stood under the trapdoor, fighting a frown. "Can we please go up, Mr. Huntley? Maybe there's clues up there."

"Show it to him, so he stops asking." Nate flung up his hands.

Sage whispered fiercely, "no."

"Not today, Mr. Emery, Mr. Clark. I think it's time for us to go. Miss Emery looks like she could use a rest." Huntley took her arm, his clasp solid. And warm. How was that possible? This strange world she'd entered had no rules.

Sage walked with Huntley toward the stairs, her head dizzy. "Come quickly, boys. We'll visit again." Or she would. She had to keep one toe in the manor. Could she be important enough to free them all?

* * *

Dad smiled as Patrick with Nate climbed onto the large stones in front of the Rock Temple in what was left of the Maolis Gardens. The structure, more a stone gazebo, had stacked rock pillars holding up an octangle gabled roof, weathered by ocean storms.

Sage tried to concentrate. She needed to scrub the sight of Huntley being shot by her Grandma Esther from her thoughts. For this moment, she wanted to shed the manor from her mind, too.

"Some call this the Witch House," Dad said. "Fredrick Tudor built it so people could view the ocean from an elegant observation edifice."

"Wasn't he called the Ice King?" Sage glanced around. Did his ghost haunt this area? They were out today to please her parents. Fresh air and no Lakeluster House, yet she felt restless, as if she should, despite herself, be doing something important at the manor.

"About 1860 he invented a way to ship ice to warm places, like India. He's also known for planting fruit trees on Nahant and encouraging others to do so." Dad nodded, hands raised. "He improved this island."

"Isn't there a tale a woman from Salem hid around here to escape the witch trials?" Sage tried to recall what she'd learned in history class. "I guess that's why it's called the Witch House." Wasn't that what their cottage was called? How strange.

"In the 1600s, a woman named Sarah I believe; but it's just a legend." Dad chuckled. "She supposedly hid under this rock base in a cave long before this structure was built, but there isn't much room."

Now *there* was a possibility of a ghost. Sage gripped her arms. Would she forever be the haunted one? Or was she possessed? *No, never!*

She should be enjoying this time with her father, glad she still had a father who decided his family was more important than anything else.

"I'm king of the world!" Patrick stood on a railing, arms in the air.

"Please get down before that old wood collapses," Dad said, his voice commanding but rarely stern.

"He's gassing. I'm waiting for him to fall on his face." Nate laughed.

"Boys, let's walk through the former gardens." Dad waved them over. He stepped into the weeds that once held the garden. "Tudor, a bit eccentric, built a dance hall and teahouse made of seashells among his fruit trees and flowers. He had a lion carved into the cliffside, and murals painted of sea serpents. His widow had an amusement park created, and people ferried over to visit from the mainland."

"Is this our history lesson, Dad?" Nate asked, shoulders slumped.

"It is. The widow willed the gardens to Nahant, but the taxpayers wouldn't support it, and the area went to ruin." Dad shook his head. "Much of this is now private land, so we need to be discreet."

They'd visited here before with their mom, and she and Lilah, with other friends, had roamed about; but Sage didn't want to spoil Dad's fun. She felt closer to him today— and that was a positive thing.

"I'm not good at history. I think we came here on a field trip." Patrick snatched up a rock, looking about to throw it. Then apparently he changed his mind and dropped it in the dirt.

"So, everything is okay with our family?" she asked Dad in a low voice.

"Yes, dear. I've apologized sincerely to your mother. I love all of you. Please don't worry." He rubbed her shoulder, his smile sad.

"What are you whispering about?" Nate ran over, his gaze searching.

"What a fine group we are, son. A wonderful family." Dad grasped his shoulder. "Let's walk down to the beach and look for interesting sea life." He started off, the breeze tugging at his checkered Bermuda shorts. "You kids need to broaden your horizons."

"Maybe a sea serpent!" Patrick jogged after them. "Something dangerous."

"Next week we can visit the Boston Museum of Science, and drop in on my parents."

Sage smiled. Her grandparents in Boston were nice people with no murderers in the family.

Suddenly, she felt a ripple at the back of her neck and turned. A small woman in a plain long dress and apron, her hair covered by a white coif, was slipping under the rock base of the temple. She gave Sage a quick look over her shoulder. "Be cautioned and take care of thyself, young miss." she said, then disappeared into the cave.

Sage winced. Was that Sarah? Would ghosts be everywhere she went from now on? And warning her about the danger ahead?

* * *

Traipsing through the woods, the pine scent sharp in the humid air, Sage watched the sky cloud up. "Are you sure you want to do this?"

Lilah, behind her on the narrow path, laughed. It sounded a little nervous. "I need to. I haven't been out here since...since after the police investigated."

At loud honking, they turned to see Mrs. Desmond herding her flock of geese down another path in the opposite direction. She was a common occurrence on Nahant. The girls waved; she waved back. The geese fluttered and flapped around her in a cloud of white.

Sage and Lilah continued to walk until the manor came into view. Sage felt a prickle along her shoulders. She hated to bring her friend into this bizarre—but *hers* to experience—situation. She hadn't been back for four days since Huntley's 'murder.' How could she look at him the same way as before? She didn't dare tell Lilah the current butler was the man her relative shot a century ago.

She'd also said nothing about the Rock Temple excursion the day before—and the colonial ghost's warning before dashing into a cave. Anywhere around her a gauzy shape could appear, keeping her on edge. Yet after talking to her dad, she felt better about her family.

"The house looks like it's about to sag into the ground." Lilah studied the decrepit manor with its peeling purple paint. "I can't believe anyone lives there. And you go in and visit? To see your ghostly friends."

"The place isn't so bad inside." Sage wondered if they were all ghosts, even Miss Dora. And what about Huntley's remark about her being connected to the family? Part of her wanted to stay away, but most of her couldn't. Was she brave or stupid? She clenched her shoulder muscles and turned to the oak tree. "It's the second largest branch."

"I know. That's where they found him." Lilah walked to the branch next to where the swing hung.

They both moved closer, through sweet pepperbush and clover, staring up at the limb. "Yeah. There's a scrape on the bark where the rope must have been looped." Sage fought a tremor.

Lilah stood on tiptoes. "I can see it. Poor Mr. Saunders. He was my favorite teacher. He treated us like adults." Her friend then studied her. "Do these ghosts you talk to tell you what happened to him?"

"No. It's the one thing I haven't learned." Sage heard the small doubt in Lilah's question. "He was kind, funny, and made history come alive."

Lilah stepped near the reeds, among shadbush and elderberry, her hands on the hips of her ripped shorts. Her blonde hair ruffled in the light breeze. "He was killed just for asking questions and wanting to write a book? Why didn't they order him to simply leave them alone? It's like he was attacked and mangled by an animal. But how can an animal hang someone? Unless something or someone else did that."

Sage kept glancing at the manor. Was Huntley watching them? "You're right. Some places, people, do awful things to hide their secrets." *Some horrible creatures with the ability to shift in shape!* Was their teacher skinned for extra punishment? "It's something I'm still trying—"

"Look!" Lilah walked toward the pond and bent down. She pulled a muddy wad of material from the weeds. She shook it out.

"An apron. A child's apron." It stank of mold and damp foliage.

Sage came beside her, crunching through the reeds. Bella's? A rusty stain covered the apron's lower edges. Blood? Her skin crawled.

"Ew. That looks like blood. Weren't there other deaths mentioned about this place? My grandpa once talked about people vanishing." Lilah stared at her with anxious eyes. "We should take this to the police."

"*No.* Leave it here." Sage snatched the material, wondering why it hadn't rotted. Again, the past and present collided. She tossed the apron into the foliage where Lilah found it. "The girl will want it back."

A group of monarch butterflies fluttered into the air, their orange bodies a contrast to the gray sky.

"What are you talking about? What girl?" Lilah's mouth twisted. "Another ghost? You did say there was a child."

"You're starting not to believe me." Sage filled with disgust that Bella might have been injured before Harrison Brubaker pushed her into the pond. And sadness that Lilah might distrust her. "There was a little girl."

"But this child was hurt. It's wrong. When could it have happened?" Lilah stared down at the apron and poked at it with her sandal, her toes curling.

The clouds overhead gathered in a darkening mass. The breeze picked up.

"It was about a hundred and fifty years ago. There's nothing we can do now." Sage struggled to sound reasonable. *In the 1800s!*

"How can you be sure? Oh, this is too creepy." Lilah held out her hand. "I felt a raindrop. But, Sage, are you okay?"

"How can I be when I talk to ghosts? I know terrible things." Sage couldn't keep the snarkiness from her tone. *I watched my Grandma Esther kill her boyfriend.* "Let's go."

She turned and trudged back, away from the pond. The attic window of the manor creaked open. Was the creature observing them? A hairy paw with long nails slid out, then swiftly withdrew. She froze, unsure of what she'd seen.

Lilah reached her. More raindrops fell. "Really, are you okay?"

"As okay as I can be." Sage grabbed her friend's hand. "Let's hurry home."

"Don't get so heated." Lilah squeezed her fingers. "I worry about you."

"I'm sorry I was salty." Sage feared it was too late with the heated. It tingled through her and encircled her brain. But was there a purpose behind it she hadn't yet figured out? They headed for the woods.

Then Lilah stopped, chin raised. "Did you hear that?"

Sage hesitated, hearing the patter of rain on the birch tree leaves. The dampness on her flimsy blouse made her squirm. "What?"

"A child laughing." Lilah met her gaze. "Is it real?"

"Are you joining the crazy club?" Sage strained to listen. Yes, there it was, laughter. Could it be Bella? But why would Lilah hear her? Did the dimensions crack open now and then? Sage's pulse jumped. She dragged Lilah farther into the woods, their feet scuffing over the dirt that turned to mud. "We're going to my house to dry off."

* * *

Jacob:
Sage knows now, that clever girl. She, too, is a part of this house, but she doesn't yet know her blood connection. She'll be relentless from now on. She must be the one chosen to release the evil in this manner. So young, is she up to it? I didn't think so at first. Now, I see that it's true. Bella knew, that's why she showed her what happened that day. My biggest shame come back to destroy me. People don't think of the consequences of their actions, how it affects others. How others can be driven beyond sanity. I only hope Sage will survive what might be coming. I don't want her to turn into one of us.

Chapter 19

In her room the next day, after a bad night trying to sleep, Sage opened the Halloween Horror Make-up kit her mom had recently ordered for her.

She placed the practice head on her small desk and laid out the paints, latex, spirit gum, and other items that came with it. In her dreams, she'd seen a creature stalking closer to her—waking her with a start—and now felt compelled to recreate it.

Spreading the latex like skin, she molded lumps on the head. She painted yellow eyes ringed with black, and an ugly mouth in a sneer, with brown fangs. The strong chemical smells made her eyes water. She pushed her thumbs into the latex to fashion more grooves and jagged edges, then painted the bumpy skull a rusty brown.

She slid her chair back, wiping her hands on a cloth. It looked grotesque, but close to what she'd dreamed about. She clenched her teeth. Was this the thing hiding in the attic? Greed, Pride, and Wrath. How about Envy? Did the creature want control of the house, jealous of anyone who broke the privacy? That's why Mr. Saunders...

Sage's breath sharpened; she was also poking into the manor's past, exposing its sins.

Everyone had sins! Her family had their own. Her dad and Patrick's both guilty of Lust. So were Jacob Huntley and Grandma Esther. Then Envy at losing him drove her ancestor to Wrath. Huntley, was he *really* dead? Sage's shoulders bunched. What was her sin? Was being "nosy" considered one? Mr. Saunders might think so.

Maybe she should speak to Mrs. Crippin, the so-called village witch. Just to see if she was fake or had some information. What do you do with monsters?

After a quick knock, her mother entered with a basket of laundry. "Oh, dear. What is that?"

"I'm not sure yet." Sage tried to keep her voice light. "I'm experimenting."

Jenny set the basket on the bed. "I wish you'd let me buy you the pretty make-up kit. Are you planning to do horror shows?"

"Maybe. In the theater, I'll need all kinds of skills." The thing seemed to stare right into her, sending icicles through her veins. "I'll do the pretty faces, too."

Jenny removed folded underwear, bras, and socks from the basket and set them on the bed. "Are you finished with your visits to Lakeluster House?"

A strange alarm rose inside Sage. A sense of loss—the odd connection she had to Lakeluster. She kept her voice even. "No, not yet."

"But you said you solved the murder, though not how you did that. I hope you didn't cause any problems with asking too many questions." Her voice, full of worry, implied she wanted details.

"I didn't, Mom." Sage's cheeks burned and she pressed her wrists on her thighs. Only a shock over the truth!

"There were hints in the diary." Her mom shook her head. "I just couldn't believe my grandmother received messages from her dead mother, so I quit reading it. My grandfather told her to stop making such outrageous claims. They'd argue over it."

At least by finding the pistol, as written in the diary, Sage was convinced her great grandmother *was* really communicating with her mother.

Sage turned to fully face her mom, thinking she herself must be cray-cray. "I want to keep visiting. I like...taking tea with Miss Dora. She seems lonely out there." The lie, coated with guilt, came too easily.

"That's sweet, but you should spend time with kids your own age." Jenny sat on the bed, her expression serious. "Ride your bike, enjoy the summer. The pool in town is open."

"And full of tourists." Sage hated the way she looked in her swimsuit. "Lilah and I might go swimming. Our other friends are off on vacation." She thought of Lilah hearing a child's laughter. Maybe it was a different child, and not Bella.

"Big changes are coming with you entering high school. When summer is over, I hope you concentrate on that." Her mom met her gaze steadily. "Do you have any concerns or worries you'd like to talk about?"

"Sure. I will, promise." Sage smiled, hoping it looked warm. Her mother wouldn't like her concerns that had nothing to do with school. "I'd like to grow taller."

Jenny laughed, her dark hair brushing her shoulders. "I'm afraid you've taken after me in that respect. We're doomed to be short."

Doomed. There was a word Sage didn't care for.

Sage shifted in the chair. She once wished she could discuss her recent problems, talking to ghosts, murder, and feel her mom's warm embrace and soothing words. But she realized she'd upset her and needed to deal with it on her own. Her big step into being a woman, or almost a woman. "We'll talk later."

"Okay. Just so you know, I'm available for mother-daughter discussions." Jenny stood and picked up the basket, her gaze thoughtful. "We still need to go shopping on the mainland to get you new clothes."

"Mom, about you and Dad. Have you forgiven him completely now?" Sage wasn't sure why she opened this subject.

"It was difficult. But it's the only way to move on. He's ashamed and sad about what happened." Her mom's eyes filled with emotion. "We need to heal."

"Good. I want us to heal. You and Dad belong together."

"You know I met your dad in college in Boston. He in education, me in business. We were so young. I never thought we'd end up dating, seriously. But we did." Her mom looked wistful. "He swept me off my feet, as they say." Now a smile tugged at her lips. "He made me laugh. Yet my parents thought him too...theatrical."

"That sounds like Dad. Always putting on a show." Sage smiled. But not a braggart, she almost said. Once she thought his antics entertaining, but as she grew...

"We waited, months, before planning our wedding. My parents loved him by then. And I was hooked. The small-town girl and the big city man." Jenny rocked the basket.

"And you talked him into moving out here." Into their historic little cottage, her mom's family place, Sage mused. The place not good enough for Patrick's dad, since Aunt Theresa had first dibs on the cottage as the oldest.

"Your father loves it here. Good fishing, the beaches. Well, don't worry about us. We'll talk more about shopping, soon."

Jenny pressed Sage's shoulder, then left the room, closing the door.

Sage sighed. At least she could be hopeful her family remained intact. Still, she felt sad to lie to her mother about her interests in the manor. She turned to the creature. Did it look scarier than before? She picked up her brush, dabbed it into red paint, and made blood drip from its jaws. *Ugh.* What could she do about this monster—if it really existed? A silver bullet? Or were those just for werewolves?

Had the creature's lips moved into more of a snarl. No, *that's too gross!* She swallowed slowly.

Cleaning her hands with hand sanitizer, everyone's friend during Covid, she opened her desk drawer. She pulled out the diary written by her Great-Grandmother Barbara. The poor woman, not believed by anyone. Would Sage end up like that as a granny?

She flipped through the pages, scanning for information.

After detailing the burial of the pistol, her great-grandma talked more about the voice from her mom, Esther, who kept haunting her.

"Mother laments what she's done, and wails this into my brain. *Jacob follows me, even after death. I look into his blue eyes. He seems so present, but I know he can't be. My heart is broken. The detectives haven't figured out who shot him. His body was discovered in a former servant's tiny bedroom on the third floor. There is cruel gossip about my attachment to him. I pretend to be a frail woman who could never fire a gun. I must leave this place and find work elsewhere.*

Will he follow me there, or remain here, trapped in the manor? When I die, will I be forced to return to Lakeluster House for my sins? To walk its halls, forever in purgatory.

Sage closed the diary, her fingers shaking. Were they all prisoners of the manor? How could she help them, and not endanger herself?

Chapter 20

Miss Dora sat on a white, wrought-iron chair in the rear garden, a place Sage hardly recognized. She'd been told by Huntley at the front door to come around to the back.

Miss Dora tipped up the brim of her wide straw hat, her eyes shaded by sunglasses. She grinned. "I'm so pleased you've come to visit us, Miss Emery."

"I'm happy to be here, Miss." Sage stared around at the garden. The weeds had been cleared out, and new plants planted. "It's all changed." And so quickly.

"We have shrubs of Arrowood and Bearberry. Bigleaf Hydrangea with the purple flowers," Miss Dora said, pride in her voice.

"Black cherry and White Cedar have been rooted along the edges." Huntley indicated the saplings.

Sage inhaled the green scents as she walked on the new gravel path, feet crunching. The early afternoon air was less humid for once. "This looks great."

The fountain was cleaned out, but the poor headless statue still appeared sad—or as sad as you can be without a face.

"I should have invited you and your chums over since you're adept at digging holes," Huntley said as he walked with her.

Sage fought a smile. She had trouble meeting his eyes, knowing what she knew about him from nearly a week past. Yet here he stood, as solid as anyone else.

"What did you find in your hole-digging?" he asked, voice low.

"I bet you already know." She gave him a quick glance, relieved no blood covered his shirt.

"You've grown so clever, after what you witnessed. You're a brave young lady." He looked even younger today, and slimmer. His tone was almost a compliment. Was he somehow changing to the younger Jacob?

"I guessed a lot before that." Sage hated to boast, but his scrutiny and transforming body unnerved her. Was the sin of Pride creeping into her? Since meeting Bella, the idea of sins was too much on her mind. She felt a prick of fear. Of helplessness—as if she walked a tightrope, trying to balance.

"I thought you'd be finished with us, now that you've seen what your Grandmother Esther did, in all its ugly detail." He was slightly taunting her.

But how could you be dead? she wanted to demand. Why did she feel betrayed? Had she come back here to study him again? Or for a bigger purpose that churned in her mind? A purpose she wasn't sure she could handle—if she understood it.

"I never meant to hurt her. I was a selfish lad then." He sounded remorseful. "I wasn't ready or able to settle down, and now I never will. Though servants, like a manservant, seldom started their own families. They remained tied to their master until pensioned off, if lucky."

Sadness enveloped her. "I'm sorry she did what she did. You could have left Lawrence and had a family, later, if you hadn't been—"

"Perhaps. But the fates had other ideas. I might have been a less than devoted husband and father." He gave a quick wistful smile.

Patrick's dad's face flashed into her mind. His barking laugh, his bragging.

"How can you seem so...real? Like an actual person?" She nearly put her hand on his shoulder; would it slide right through? Yet he'd taken her arm before and he felt solid. "I don't understand that."

"That's my secret, Miss Emery." His gaze twinkled.

"How did you end up with Miss Dora?" she asked, flicking a glance in that person's direction.

"I wanted to return here, or was compelled to. I knew she would return one day. Plus she needed my guidance."

"Does she know..." Sage couldn't finish. Her mouth went dry.

A movement to her right made Sage look. At the end of the garden, a young woman in a long peach-colored dress with a huge bow in the back, was bent over picking flowers. She wore a small straw hat over blonde hair, two tight ringlets dangling on her cheeks. Sage hadn't even noticed the flowers before this. She had seen this woman before, pulling weeds the evening of the pistol search, before she'd hurried away. The woman glanced over at her now, her smile sad.

"Don't chatter over there. I am hard of hearing," Miss Dora called. "Huntley, serve lemonade to our visitor."

"Right away, ma'am." Huntley swept out his hand. "After you, Miss Emery."

Sage walked back and sat in the other hard chair, a small wrought-iron table between them. Huntley entered the manor.

"I've put off so much, my dear." Miss Dora spread out her age-spotted hands. "It was about time we cleaned out this garden."

"It looks pretty." Sage still didn't feel comfortable, as if they were all waiting for something eerie to happen. Or more eerie than what had already happened. She didn't know who was real and who wasn't. She perched on the edge of the chair, in case she had to quickly leave. Yet she wanted answers—and needed courage. "Who is the blonde lady picking flowers?"

"There's no one else here." Miss Dora tipped up her straw hat. "This house, once full of life, is lonely now. You know, I once had a beau. But I broke off our engagement.”

Sage was surprised by this topic, remembering a bo was a boyfriend. And who *was* the lady in peach? Another ghost as she suspected? Somehow, she knew she’d visited today because she was meant to see her. Sage pressed on her temples. “Oh, no engagement? Why did you break it off?”

“Because men like to tell you what to do.” The woman giggled. “I was strong-minded then. And wanted my freedom. I owned a flower shop in England for a while. A happy life until my brothers were killed in the war. Then I took care of my invalid parents.”

“Real nice,” Sage said. “The flower shop, not about your brothers. I’m sorry you lost them.” She didn’t ask which war, leery of the answer.

“Death stalks us all.” Miss Dora said it so airily.

“I don’t think of boys yet,” Sage said to change the subject. And now ghosts filled her senses, far too many, crowding everything else out.

“That’s good. Take your time on that count. In these days, women don’t even need to marry. It was a risk in my youth.” Miss Dora sat up straighter in her loose-fitting blue gown. She wore sandals over thick stockings. She stared over the yard. “Maybe we can find the head for that poor statue.”

Sage glanced at the fountain, then couldn't resist looking up at the attic window. Would it open like last time? Would the creature resemble her creation?

Miss Dora pulled down her sunglasses and eyed Sage in a sharper way than ever before. "Do you seek something? Something best left ignored or forgotten? If that's possible."

"I've found a...lot here." Sage ached to ask if the woman knew her butler was a ghost. Should she forget the creature? Or would it haunt her dreams? Bella slid into her thoughts. A child trapped. She gripped the knees of her khaki Bermuda shorts.

"My mother once told me the manor was full of sin." The old woman winked. "I think my sin lately is Sloth."

Huntley returned with a tray with two glasses. He set it on the small table. He handed one to each of them. Sage sipped the tart liquid.

"What do you do about sins?" Sage asked. *What dwells in the attic?* She wanted to ask.

Huntley gave her a wry smile. "Perhaps 'curiosity' should be a sin. It did kill the cat, as the old saying goes."

"Don't tease the girl. She's finding her reason for coming in the first place." Miss Dora drank from her glass. "Let's hope she figures it out. It may be the only way."

Huntley frowned, as if he didn't want her to pursue anything.

Sage shifted in the chair. This woman seemed so different from the Miss Dora she'd met before. Everyone was changing.

Miss Dora set down her glass. Something dripped from her hair, a red glistening liquid. Blood again? Sage opened her mouth to warn her, but the drips vanished, just like before. Huntly was staring off the other way.

Sage held her breath. She really was losing her mind. What did these visions of wounds mean? What injury had the woman suffered? Miss Dora might also be a ghost! Sage's stomach clenched, but she had no urge to leave. She *must* figure all this out.

* * *

A bell tinkled as Sage entered Witchy Wiles: Crippin's Souvenirs and Gifts, just off Nahant Road. The small shop smelled of jasmine, orange, and blackberry. Lilah had suggested Sage come here, to consult the "village witch." But Sage wasn't certain how anyone could help with the problem at the manor.

Sage's mom always called the owner a strange woman who fancied herself a Wiccan. But it was a pink-painted, glowing place. Hardly a witch's den.

Wide-cheeked Mrs. Crippin, with her dyed, burgundy-colored hair, stood behind the counter. She came out from behind it. "Oh, my, is this Miss Sage Emery, Jenny's girl, grown so big?"

The bracelets on her arms clinked together, her plump fingers sporting garish rings. She flipped her long curls behind the shoulder of her flowing, boldly flowered gown, a garden of yellows and pinks on a green background.

"Good afternoon, Mrs. Crippin." Sage inspected the shelves of scented candles, polished stones, and crystals, along with cross-stitched dolphin pillows that said, "Welcome to Nahant." And, "Nahant's the Beach."

The walls were hung with watercolor scenes of the island. Or frames holding collections of shells. Tiny bottles of herbal scents and perfumes sat on an antique buffet. Only a maroon pentagram high up behind the counter hinted at any witchy activity the owner bragged about.

"What may I do for you?" The woman wore tons of make-up, her lips scarlet, her false eyelashes too thick, but with the lines around her eyes she still looked about fifty.

Sage hesitated, picking up a pillow then putting it back. She stepped to the counter. Mrs. Crippin swished back behind it.

"I...wondered...what do you know about Lakeluster house?"

The woman's eyes widened for a second. "Probably as much as anyone."

"My Grandma Esther killed a man there." Sage's words came out blunter than she wished.

"So, you're aware of that history." Mrs. Crippin arranged scented soaps in a basket on the counter. "Quite the scandal it was."

"I visit there. I've learned a lot." Sage picked up a lavender soap and sniffed the sweet, flowery aroma.

"Whom do you speak to there?" The woman clicked her rings together. One had the face of a skull. Another a dragon. "I heard about the returning residents; or were they there all along?"

"Miss Dora Brubaker and her butler, Huntley." Sage was still uneasy about Huntley and probably Miss Dora being ghosts.

"It seems to me, the young man killed by your relative was also named Huntley."

"Yes. An ancestor." Sage sounded too defensive.

"Perhaps that's true." Mrs. Crippin's tone dug under Sage's skin. "The manor has a long, sad past. Then Mr. Saunders' death added to it."

"What do you know about the history?" Sage leaned her elbow on the counter.

"My dear husband, Walter, when he was alive of course, warned me to stay out of the manor's business. Men are uncomfortable with female power. He insisted we start this shop to keep me out of mischief.

"My family has been on Nahant since the 1600s. We were all cunning women. And one of my ancestors lived in your cottage. A healer." Mrs. Crippin rearranged some artificial flowers with silk butterflies in a wide vase. "History? This place is full of it. A native named Poquanum sold Nahant to Thomas Dexter in 1630, but it seems more a swindle on Dexter's part than a sale. The tribe might have cursed the island."

"I learned that in school. Well, not the curse part." That was long before the road was built, when people in vehicles or horses could only come here at low tide.

"At least the later settlers planted trees after the earlier ones cut them down for pasture. They'd left this island barren." Mrs. Crippin smiled, eyes glinting. "Did you know a sea serpent once appeared in these waters? My ancestor wrote about this in her spell—cookery book."

A sea serpent. Sage wasn't certain she wanted to go there. She had enough strangeness happening. "What about the Brubakers? What do you know of them?"

"An outsider, Harrison Brubaker was not a kind man." The woman's brow furrowed. "And that's an understatement. He was raised by strict, cold parents, it's said. He only cared about making money, and his legacy, no matter whom he hurt. Hiding his insecurities, I suppose."

"I have heard awful things about him."
Sage saddened and thought of Bella, the
blood on the apron Lilah found.

"My ancestor had troubling visions
about Lakeluster but kept them inside our
family." Mrs. Crippin twirled her fingers in
the air. "The Salem Witch trials hung over
all their heads from past times."

"I've heard the stories; and visited
Salem. A terrible time for women." Sage
was relieved to live in a time where she had
rights. She started to warm to Mrs. Crippin.

"Women must fight twice as hard as
men to prevail. You look quite earnest. Does
your mother approve of your involvement
there?" Mrs. Crippin picked up a small
bottle from behind the counter. She opened
it. "This is Frankincense. It helps wisdom
and concentration." She lifted it toward
Sage.

"My mom doesn't really approve." Sage
sniffed the potion. It smelled of spicy tree
bark.

"I shouldn't do this, but you seem in
great need." Mrs. Crippin put some on her
finger and rubbed it on her forehead,
leaving a glistening streak. She closed her
eyes, her eyelashes like spiders on her
cheeks. She hummed a strange tune. "I see
a child near water. Distress. But first, a
lonely woman who drinks a fouled brew.
Death all around. I know of these people."

Sage's heart throbbed. "What else?"

The woman stared at her. "None of this surprises you. You've met with spirits, haven't you?"

Sage filled with excitement that Mrs. Crippin certainly seemed to be a witch, or at least a woman with some deep knowledge. Would Sage encounter werewolves and invading zombies next? Her world was spinning. "I...hate to say."

"Oh, child, you have an aura. I see forms of it. Hmmm. You appear to have the sight, a special gift." Mrs. Crippin's gaze sharpened. "A gift or a plague, I should admit. You must use it carefully."

Sage gripped the counter. "I'm not sure. This gift just happened to me. What do you know about sins, sins that turned into...more?"

"Aha. The ugliest secret of the manor." The woman thrust up her arm, bracelets jangling. "A myth? An evil. I shouldn't tell you, you're so young."

"Please. I need help." Sage's voice rasped in desperation. Was she wasting her time?

"Didn't your relative delve into the spiritual world? Barbara was her name. Oh, never mind. The path you've chosen..." Mrs. Crippin shook her head, her burgundy hair rustling. "But have you actually seen it?"

"No." Unless it was the shapeshifter. "And I didn't choose any path. But I think I need to get rid of it," Sage whispered as her skin goose bumped. Would this help the trapped people to leave the manor? To go to Heaven? If that was what they wanted.

Mrs. Crippin narrowed her eyes. "That's a momentous task. A very dangerous one. The sin-filled creature has had many years to evolve. The denial of the people there gave it fuel. Your great-great grandmother added to it. The young man she murdered. Do you have the tenacity, the bravery?"

The door opened as the bell tinkled behind Sage. A couple dressed in shorts and tank tops walked in, their voices breezy.

"I think I do." Sage strained to hide her doubts.

Mrs. Crippin grasped her wrist. "Be careful. And I don't encourage you to do anything. Come back next week. I might have just the right mixture for you—and the way to accomplish it. This will take some research." She turned to the customers with a smile. "Welcome; how may I help you?"

Sage hurried from the shop, wondering what madness she was tumbling into now. Yet it stirred her on, no matter how frightening.

Chapter 21

Sage wandered down a different, narrower path, through the woods, relieved the boys had gone with her dad to the movies. An action movie Sage didn't care to see, though it took a lot of persuading for her dad to let her stay home. Her mom was with her garden club. Sage needed to clear her head, alone.

Her mind kept pondering over her conversation the day before with Mrs. Crippin. Could the so-called witch help her?

Ending up at the other end of the pond, she viewed the manor across the scummy water. A bird chirped from the oak tree. Insects swirled up from the bushes and she swiped them away. The mid-afternoon air felt sticky on her skin.

She stared up at the attic window. Was anyone watching her? She felt possessive of this place, supposedly 'chosen' to help the inhabitants. But could it all be a mistake?

"Sage, have you come to join me in my research?"

Startled, she whipped around. Mr. Saunders stood there. All in one piece, in his khaki pants and yellow collared pullover shirt. He looked so normal, she stifled her gasp. Another hallucination? A ghost?

"You can't be here, Mr. Saunders," was all she could manage through a tight throat. *You're dead. Yet the dead seem everywhere.*

"Nonsense." He hooked his hands on his belt. A short man, with a chubby face and body, his smile held its usual warmth. His black-rimmed glasses perched on a small nose. "I'm writing a history on the property, the manor house. I'm only exploring."

Her heart squeezed. Was this the shapeshifter trying to trick her?

"Have...have you spoken to the people inside?" She resisted taking a step backwards, in case he was the monster. Her stomach gurgled and she pressed her fingers on it. She mustn't act afraid.

"Not yet. No one is ever home when I knock." He gazed around. "A shame they let this place fall to ruin. Brubaker's first wife brought more property into the marriage. But his second wife gave him the children he wanted. There were rumors his first wife was poisoned."

"Poisoned? That's awful." Was the first wife a ghost lost in the manor? The woman in the peach dress? Sage needed to ask Bella. She also figured this Mr. Saunders was an earlier version, before he spoke to Huntley. How sharp she'd become when it came to ghosts.

She wanted to warn him not to ask too many questions or he'd anger something more dangerous than he could ever imagine. But wasn't it too late?

"I suppose I shouldn't mention such things to a girl your age." A sudden breeze ruffled his brown hair, thinning on top.

"You'll never believe what I've already seen." She stretched taller. "I've grown up a lot this summer."

"I see that you have. Are you also interested in the manor? The Brubakers came over from England in the 1800s. Harrison Brubaker wanted to cash in on the bustling tourist trade here on Nahant. His hotel was one of many. But his was the largest, the more extravagant. It burned down in the 1950s. His family had made their fortune in steam engines."

"I hear he wasn't a kind man." Sage couldn't believe she was standing here, talking to Mr. Saunders, a man brutally murdered. Of course, she'd already witnessed her own great-great-grandmother shoot Huntley to death. Her heartbeat sped up. Would her life ever return to normal?

"Harrison was callous and calculating by all accounts. His parents were unhappily married and took their bitterness out on the children. He built his monstrosity of a house over a Native American holy place. Many believe that put a curse on the house. The Wampanoag tribe was especially upset." Mr. Saunders shrugged. "If you believe in such things as curses. And the indigenous people had no rights back then. So much happened here. During Prohibition, Harrison's descendants held alcohol parties in what was a secret passage."

Sage almost admitted she'd been in that passage. "Prohibition, that's when alcohol was against the law, right?"

"Yes, that's right. You've paid attention in history class. The Brubakers were always a boisterous, though conniving family." He smiled at her. "I enjoy enriching young people's minds. My parents taught me to seek to learn, and share that learning."

"And that's why you became a teacher." She still couldn't believe she was having this conversation.

"Yes." He looked away, then turned to look at her again, but something had changed. A large scratch covered one of his cheeks.

She took a long, deep breath. Should she leave now? Saunders could be about to trick her. Ghost or monster?

"You look scared. What's the matter?" A trickle of blood dribbled down the other side of his face.

"Have you seen it? The creature? You must have. Can't you feel that...the scratch, the blood?" She pointed a finger, her hand shaking. His ghost was switching to a more recent version. The version on his last day alive.

He smiled. "I don't feel anything. And what do you know of the creature?" His voice turned jittery. "I, too, have seen what shouldn't be seen."

Then his skin began to peel off his face, his clothing shredded. The stink of raw meat clogged her nose.

Sage stepped farther back, swallowing a cry, then scanned the area for the monster.

Blood and raw flesh emerged on her former teacher. The shape of his skull formed, with large hollow eyes. His shredded clothes slithered off his body.

She nearly chocked as nausea rose up. She'd never seen anything so horrible.

Sage turned, relieved she had the ability, and with every effort she could gather she ran from the pond and down the trail, hiccupping with terror and trying not to vomit.

Chapter 22

Sage's mom served broiled yellowfin tuna in lemon butter sauce, jasmine rice, and green beans.

"This smells delicious, dear." Dad gave her his charming smile as he helped himself to a portion. "You've outdone yourself."

"Why, thank you." Mom blushed and nudged his shoulder with her elbow. Her parents seemed so much easier with each other—to Sage's immense relief.

Patrick took a large serving, but Nate only a small one. Fish was not his favorite.

Sage took a mid-size portion. She struggled to forget the horrible experience of seeing Mr. Saunders the day before.

Jenny returned to the kitchen and came back with warm rolls in a basket.

"You're the best cook ever," Patrick said. He grabbed and buttered a roll.

"Well, I won't tell my sister you prefer my cooking to hers." Jenny sat beside Dad. "How was your golf game today, dear?"

"I came in under par, so I'm pleased." He ate a large bite and nodded in approval. "Soon, I'll be back in the classroom and miss these lovely summer days."

Sage started to eat a bite of tuna, then put it down. It looked too raw and she nearly gagged. A man with his skin peeling off! She forced herself to taste the rice and the buttery flavor was okay, but her stomach turned over. Then she looked around at her family. They seemed so normal. And here she was, consulting with witches and talking to ghosts. Would she soon face a monster? Her life had become a scary journey.

"You're very quiet, Sage. Is your investigating at the manor through?" Dad smiled at her, though his eyes held concern.

"I'm not through. I like visiting there." She stuffed three green beans in her mouth and chewed. She had to keep going, she had business to take care of.

"Sage sneaks off without us." Nate frowned. "It's not fair."

"And it was my idea to go in the first place." Patrick flashed her a glower.

"I'd be happy if you kids found other things to do. Go swimming at the pool." Her mom ate from her plate, then sipped her iced tea. "I can buy some crafts for you to work on."

"Miss Dora needs help with her garden." Sage bristled; she needed to soften her words. Shamefully, part of her was afraid to return, in case her teacher—in skinned form—showed up again.

"Can't she afford to hire a gardener?" Dad asked. "You need to find other interests. I don't think visiting the manor anymore is a good idea."

"She likes to act important," Patrick mocked. "And tells us strange stories."

Nate nodded.

"Patrick, be nice in what you say," Dad warned. "I know your situation at home isn't ideal. And we sympathize with you."

"But we don't need to talk about it now." Jenny slathered butter on a roll. "Sage is a smart girl. She'll make the right decision."

Patrick began to eat quickly, eyes lowered.

Nate tapped his fork on his plate, lips in a pinched line.

Sage worried Nate or Patrick would tell them she spoke to ghosts. They would lock her in her room.

"I'd say a trip to the arcade at the mall on the mainland would be a fun day." Dad scooped up more rice.

Sage stirred the food on her plate, fast losing her appetite as she felt pushed into a corner. They'd never understand her purpose. She wasn't the same person she was before. She tugged more and more against the authority of her parents. "I'd still like to go to Lakeluster. Miss Dora offered to pay me to help."

"I had no idea you were so interested in gardening." Jenny eyed her warily.

"I'm...changing. Finding new interests, like you said." Sage hated the lies but had no choice. She gripped her fork so tight, it stung her skin.

I have a monster to kill!

* * *

Inside the manor the next afternoon, unable to escape the boys, though sneaking off while her mom and dad had gone shopping for groceries, Sage scrutinized Huntley. He still looked like a living person to her. And he appeared closer to his older self. A relief. But how did ghosts 'age'? Bella seemed stuck at the age she died.

"Yes, I'm here to visit. Again. If I can." Sage forced a smile. Bella had slipped into her dreams the night before, asking her to come.

Huntley arched an eyebrow. "I'm well aware of why you are here. Still, I don't exactly consent to these further explorations."

"Why *are* we here?" Patrick crossed his arms. "Sage keeps leaving us out. She knows things but won't talk about it."

"She says she talks to ghosts. Can she prove it?" Nate glared at her. "Did you see Grandma Esther? Or are you teasing?"

"Why can't *we* see her?" Patrick demanded. "You must be lying. You're not so special. And what about Mr. Saunders? Did you find out what happened to him?"

Sage held her breath; her chest tightened. "This...this is why I don't like

190

bringing you with me." She swallowed her frustration, anxious to go upstairs.

"Young men, stop being rude to your sister. You must learn decorum." Huntley grimaced. He lowered his brows. "Would you like to see the basement? There are interesting items down there. Famously used in the past for torture."

"Is it like a dungeon?" Nate asked, eyes shining.

"Harrison Brubaker was quite the collector." Huntley gave them a sly smile. "There's a Tongue Tearer and Thumbscrews."

"Wow! I would go. But Nate and Sage might be too afraid." Patrick's face lit up as he smirked.

"Miss Emery will have tea with Miss Dora. Upstairs this time." Huntley winked at her.

Sage somehow knew he meant for her to meet with Bella. And she trusted him to protect them...sort of. Could ghosts be trusted? "Yes, thanks."

"I won't be afraid. I'm growing up." Nate scowled. "I'm going to be a forensic scientist. Show me the torture, too."

"I want to coach football, tough and rough," Patrick said, flexing his arm muscles.

"Then let us leave your sister and proceed to the downstairs." Huntley turned to Sage. "Your company awaits." He leaned close to her and whispered, "Be very cautious."

Patrick muttered, "I could use torture on my dad's new almost-wife. Thumbscrews, yeah."

Nate laughed.

Sage waved them both away, then mounted the stairs as the butler hustled the boys in another direction.

When she reached the landing, she knew she was supposed to contact Bella here, on this floor, not the usual third. Information from the dream, she wasn't sure. Would Bella talk more about the beast, and how to rid the house of it? Or was she too in fear of it?

Sage heard sounds down the hall and walked in that direction. A door on her left was ajar. She peered into a sitting room with large furniture covered in green striped material. A man was at a buffet sifting a powder into a delicate cup. Wearing a chocolate-colored vest with a gold chain dangling from a pocket, he had a long, bony face. He wore dark pants over his lengthy, thin legs.

The woman sitting on the sofa, her full skirt flared out, caught Sage's breath. She was the same blonde-haired woman Sage had seen in the garden picking flowers and pulling weeds. She had been a ghost as Sage suspected.

Someone moved up beside her. Bella. "That's Harrison Brubaker and his first wife, Nellie."

Sage's easiness with these manor ghosts grew stronger every day. And that disturbed her. What was *she* turning into?

Brubaker stirred the liquid in the cup. He turned, a broad smile on his face. "Here, my dear, this will make you feel better. Tea is a great soother, my mother always said."

The woman looked up with a frown on her delicate features. "I'm serious, Harrison. I detest this house. It's too big and drafty. Build me a pretty cottage near the sea."

"We'll discuss that, don't worry." He handed her the cup, his deep voice still too sweet, his smile too big. "Drink up for your health."

She sipped the tea, then wrinkled her nose. "It tastes strange."

He poured himself a cup and drank. "It's your imagination. The tea tastes fine to me."

Nellie started to place the cup on the low table in front of the sofa.

Mr. Saunders had said the first wife was poisoned. *Don't drink it!* Again, Sage felt useless even though these events had happened many years ago.

Brubaker lifted her hand with the cup. "No, you must finish it. You'll feel refreshed. Then we'll look at plots of land to build our cottage."

"You promise me?" She drank again from the cup.

"I do. And perhaps the sea air will improve your difficulties." His gaze hardened for a second. "Who knows? We may at last produce an heir."

Nellie's shoulders sagged. "It's been five years. I may never give you the children you want. We both want." She finished her drink. "I know it's a miserable disappointment. Oh dear, my head feels a little dizzy."

"This is when he turned and saw me," Bella said.

Brubaker did turn, his face flaming. "What are you doing there, you little brat? Stop snooping around the house."

He slammed the door shut.

Sage flinched and stepped back. "Was the door open *before* he put poison in her tea that day?"

"No, I cracked it open and saw him, after hearing them talk. I was a terrible snoop." Bella frowned. "I didn't like the way he treated his wife. She was nice to me."

"Then what happened?" Sage resisted taking the girl's hand; it might dissolve if she did. Like Huntley, she seemed so alive, but Sage knew otherwise.

"Mrs. Brubaker died that night." Bella drifted away from the door. "The next day, I was playing near the pond. I was sad, worried about what he put in the tea. I once thought I'd be a nurse when I grew up, to help people. I never got to do it."

Bella kept walking and Sage understood to follow. How tragic the child wasn't allowed to grow up. A strange sensation passed through her, like being squeezed into a narrow tunnel. The air turned cooler, a wind, and she shivered. Suddenly they stood beside the pond, a gray sky above.

Bella picked up stones and threw them in the murky water. Her apron was clean and starched.

"You, there, Bella." A man's gruff voice. Harrison Brubaker stalked through tall grass toward the child. "How long were you peeking at us yesterday?"

Bella turned, her lips pursed. "I'm sorry I did that."

"But what did you see?" Brubaker towered over her. "Tell the truth, young lady."

Sage winced at the menace in his tone. She tried to speak, but no words came out. *Why can't I talk in these situations?* But what good would it do? A different dimension, an event in the past, like Bella had said.

"I didn't see anything." Bella turned her back on him.

"I don't believe you. You're known for telling lies. My cousin should have sent you off to boarding school." He grabbed her shoulders and jerked her around, her braids lashing like whips.

Bella swung her fists at him. "Leave me alone."

He grasped one of her hands. Bella yanked it back and struck herself in the nose. Blood seeped out. She started to cry.

Sage struggled to move, but again, she was frozen in place. Her heart twisted.

"See what you've done." Brubaker shook her. "Stop that crying."

"I want my momma!" Bella wailed.

"Be quiet." He snatched her apron's edge and swiped at her nose, closing his hand over her face as if to smother her.

Bella elbowed him and ducked her head, crying louder. "I'll tell them what you did."

"You will keep your mouth shut." He shook her again. "I'm warning you. You shouldn't have been so ignorant."

Bella jerked to get free, kicking at him with her feet, her face flushed red. Brubaker lost his footing and stumbled, releasing her. She fell backwards, splashing into the pond. Flailing in the water, she sobbed. "I can't swim!"

Sage couldn't move her arms or legs to rescue her. But she knew she couldn't change what happened. Tears sprang to her eyes at her and Bella's helplessness.

Brubaker stared at the drowning child. He scratched behind his ear, as if thinking what to do.

Save her, you horrible man! Sage screamed inside her head.

But he straightened his hat and stomped off, back toward the manor.

Sage wept, her body quaking, as Bella sank into the dark waters of the pond.

Chapter 23

The breeze blew warm and salty as Sage helped her mom position the large umbrella on Nahant Beach. The miles of clean sand stretched out on the right side of the causeway, or Lynnway, that led to the mainland.

Dad pulled a bottle of sunscreen from their canvas bag. "Don't forget to slather yourself with this, even in the shade." He handed it to Mom with a soft smile.

"Thank you, dear." Jenny spread a large towel in the umbrella's shadow. "I'll sit here and read my book while you braver ones paddle in the water."

"Are we ready, brave ones? Let's go." Dad picked up his rented paddle board and headed down to the surf that lapped the sand. He wore a white t-shirt and shorts, his frame still in good shape.

"I'm more than ready." Patrick laughed and snatched up his board. "I'll be the champion."

"Me, too." Nate grabbed a board and chased after them. "Ready and a champion."

People farther to their left, tourists no doubt, kicked around a beach ball and splashed in the surf. Outsiders found it difficult to park here because most spaces were reserved for residents. A boon for the residents, Sage mused.

She picked up her board, standing it on end. She stared out at the calm ocean, but two days past filled her mind. Her watching Bella drown. Her big fear was she'd never see the ghost-girl again now that she 'saw' what happened. Sage swallowed past a thickening throat, sad for a long-dead child.

And watching Mr. Saunders shred still haunted her. Could she ever peel a potato again?

Sage ruminated on the boundary between life and death. The line seemed thin. Some slipped easily back and forth. And she was too young to think about death! Was it a black abyss, or the ability to creep in and out of people's lives?

"What's the matter, dear? You need to have fun and keep your thoughts away from anything else." Jenny opened the cooler they'd brought and pulled out a can of ice tea.

"I know. I'm off to have fun." Sage walked down the beach, hauling the board, the sand warm between her toes. She recalled when they'd come here as young children. When Aunt Theresa was with them. The sisters smiling and laughing, one blonde the other brunette. Patrick full of energy, teasing but not aggressive or rude. Nate giggling as they built sandcastles, then skipped along the surf. Carefree times, long before ghosts entered her life. Just before the move, afterwards the break between Patrick's parents. Life seemed simple, fun, and safe back then. But things changed, good or bad, no matter what you might wish for.

"Come on, Sage," Dad called. "Show us males what a courageous young lady can do."

She stepped into the cold water of Nahant Bay, the wet sand shifting beneath her feet. The sun warm on her shoulders, she wore her swimsuit with a pair of shorts.

The boys sloshed through the water until it was over waist deep. They positioned their boards, then crawled up on their bellies. Paddling with their hands, they rode the small waves back to the beach.

"These waves are too tame," Patrick said. "Can we go to the rougher surf?"

"No, these are wild enough for you kids." Dad waded farther out. He swung onto his board, balanced himself, rose on two legs, and paddled the board with a long-handled paddle. He looked like a Hawaiian god with his thick black hair blowing about his face.

Sage pushed herself into deeper water, crawled onto the board on her stomach and paddled with her hands toward shore. She liked the swaying of the board, the muscles in her arms flexing, and the calm waves, as she breathed deep to relax.

When shallow enough, she slid off the board and carried it to shore. She laughed lightly. A beautiful day to enjoy. Far away from scary troubles.

Dad and the boys soon waded to shore.

"When can we paddle standing like you?" Nate asked, steadying the board almost as tall as him.

Dad rubbed his chin. "Let's see. I think sixteen would be a good age to start." He ruffled his son's hair. Glancing at his wife, he smiled. "Were we in fine form, my love?"

Jenny laughed from the shade of her umbrella. "The most elegant of forms. The tourists are all agog."

"I'll be fifteen next month. I know I could do it." Patrick slid his board back in the water, sat on it, and pushed backwards with his feet over the ripple of waves.

"Are you sure you won't try it?" Dad walked up to her mom. "You can belly paddle."

"No thanks. For a girl born surrounded by ocean, I was never interested in water sports." Jenny raised her can of ice tea. "Now give me a ping pong table, and I'll beat you all."

Sage stuck her board upright in the sand. She trailed her fingers through her hair to dry it. Gulls squawked overhead. A large stone to her right had a crack in it. The crack widened, and she couldn't pull her gaze away. The fracture continued, in slow cracks, shaping itself into fingers that crept along the rock's surface.

Sage stiffened. Was she having sunstroke? Her parents were laughing together, paying no attention. The wind wafted across Sage's face as a pale finger near the rock rose and pointed. A voice whispered, *beware the riptide.*

She looked around in confusion. Had she lost her mind? Too late for that.

Loud splashing from farther out in the bay. Patrick. He'd gone out too far. His board bobbed in another direction.

"Dad, I think Patrick's in danger," Sage said. She ran down the beach.

"Help!" came the cry.

Dad rushed across the sand. "Don't fight it, Patrick! It's the riptide. Just relax and float. I'm coming." He sloshed into the water then dived and swam toward Patrick.

Sage stood at the water's edge, Nate beside her. Mom hurried to join them.

"Be careful!" Jenny cried.

Dad reached her cousin. "We must let it pull us along. Don't struggle." He clasped the boy's arm. "We'll float until it eases, then swim to shore."

Sage clutched her mother's arm. Nate grabbed Jenny's hand.

Other people rushed to the water's edge.

"Your father knows CPR." Jenny squeezed them both close. "If it's needed. He's also a strong swimmer."

"They'll be okay, they'll be okay," Sage said under her breath. She realized again how important her father was to her, despite his mistakes.

Time dragged. People muttered and gestured. Soon Dad was carrying Patrick from down shore, in the distance. Jenny ran to them. Dad set Patrick on his feet. She embraced Patrick. Her mom and dad hugged each other.

The others on the beach cheered.

Sage sighed in relief over a rollicking heartbeat.

Chapter 24

The day after their beach outing, Sage added bumps to the creature's forehead. Ugly knobs. Where she'd gotten this idea, she wasn't sure.

Bella's cries still disturbed her sleep. Also, the gore of Mr. Saunders. When she remembered what she witnessed, her stomach felt queasy, her heart heavy. Yesterday's events didn't help. Pointing, unattached fingers? She wriggled her shoulders.

But her parents were right. She was too involved with the manor, yet she couldn't stop, not yet. Harrison Brubaker had started the ugly sins of Pride and Greed. You'd think murder would top the list—but it wasn't even there.

"I'll get you," she told the hideous monster in front of her. "I just don't know how. Or why I was chosen." Hopefully Mrs. Crippin could help.

Am I brave enough? Am I strong enough? These doubts pinged through her brain. She shoved them away.

They expected her to come back, Miss Dora and Huntley. Or so they'd said. Though the butler cautioned her, and maybe he didn't mind being trapped in the house. Her sympathy for him had increased since seeing the murder caused by her own relative.

She pulled scissors from her desk drawer and clipped the ends of her hair. Her mom would scold her. Sage stuck the hairs into the knobs she'd just molded. What made her do that? Something briefly glimpsed in a dream?

A strange beefy odor came from the creature. She wrinkled her nose, fighting the urge to back away.

A quick knock, and Patrick opened the door. "When are we returning to the manor? You should have seen those torture devices. They were awesome— Sheesh, what the heck is that?"

She couldn't tell him this thing might dwell in the manor attic. In his reckless way, he'd demand to go there and look for it.

"Just something I made." Sage wiped her hands on a cloth.

"What do your ghosts tell you?" he asked in a taunting voice, swaggering into the room.

"You won't believe me. I saw Grandma Esther shoot her boyfriend. But I don't know who killed Mr. Saunders." She was pretty certain what it was, but something kept her from mentioning what she'd seen with her teacher. "What if it's something horrible and dangerous?"

"Like this thing you created?" He moved close to peer at it, fists on his thighs. "Pretty gross. But you saw the whole murder?"

"I might tell you more if you'd be a friend and not a bully." She stared into the creature's bloodshot eyes. Had she changed them that way? "And...so mental."

Patrick ran his fingertips over the hair. "It tickles."

"What did I just say?" Sage groaned. "Don't touch it. You're too careless. You almost drowned yesterday. My dad could have drowned, too." And what about the creeping rock-crack, and the voice? She twisted the cloth around her fingers. Were ghosts following her everywhere? She didn't like it but must figure out how to handle these changes.

"Sorry about what I did." Patrick's grin vanished. "You don't know what it's like." He walked over and sank onto the edge of her bed. "My mom cried a lot. And my dad didn't care."

"You being angry won't help. And I know some of what it's like." She remembered the arguments, her mom's sadness. Hers and Nate's confusion.

"Your dad stayed around. He was sorry, wasn't he? I still hate my dad for leaving us." Patrick swiped a lock of hair from his forehead. His dark blonde hair had grown longer, the ends curling. "His new wife is only twenty-four. Eight years older than me."

"Yeah, that was mean of him. Really selfish." Sage turned to look at her cousin. Her no-longer-an-uncle was a loud man, bossy and arrogant. She wouldn't miss him at family gatherings. "But you don't need to be hateful, too."

"Whatever." Patrick shrugged, drooping his arms between his knees. "Is that monster supposed to look like what might have killed Mr. Saunders?"

"I don't know. I dreamed this." She glanced at it again. The hairy knobs definitely made it creepier. And Patrick's guess surprised her.

"Was that the shapeshifter we saw that night on the porch? We did see that." His voice still held doubt. "You haven't been up close to it for real?"

"No. I need to talk to Mrs. Crippin again." Sage stood. She really hated having to see it too close, but the manor ghosts kept pulling at her. Her muscles clenched. Picking up the hand sanitizer, she cleaned her hands and under her fingernails.

"You got her involved?" Patrick snorted. "The wild-haired woman who thinks she's a witch."

"She knew a lot." But was there a solution from her? Sage shouldn't count on it. "You're mocking again."

"Okay." He threw up his hands. "My mom called this morning. She told me she's fine about Dad remarrying. I'll try to be, too. But I don't have to like it. Or go to the wedding."

"Good, about Aunt Theresa. I'll include you and Nate in my discoveries if you keep your word. If you try to understand." Sage probably needed their help. "I couldn't believe it either. The ghosts talking to me. Seeing Grandma Esther. It scared me."

Patrick cocked his head, a small smile. "We'll protect you. Does Grandma Esther—"

"Just behave. And listen to me." Dare she tell him Huntley was a ghost? She felt the need to keep the butler's secret. "I want to trust you. We also have to get past my parents' objections. Mom wants to meet Miss Dora." Sage didn't want her parents invading her time at the manor. And seeing the odd people who 'lived' there.

Another knock. Nate peered around the door edge. "You'll never believe what I found." His eyes flashed at the monster. "That's sooo cool."

"What did you find?" Sage asked. She really needed to get a lock on her door.

Nate held out a piece of paper. "I printed it out. You'll be shocked."

Sage took the paper. Patrick joined her.

"I was just surfing the web, and I checked English newspapers. Since Miss Dora said she lived there. I wanted to know more about her." Nate's voice spewed out in excitement. "Hurry, read it."

Sage read the article from 1973. "A Miss Dora Brubaker, formally from Nahant, Massachusetts in the United States, was killed in a car accident on a country road in Dorset. She was the last known descendant of Harrison Brubaker, a wealthy American hotel magnate from the 1800s."

"You've *got* to be joking, bro," Patrick said. "The same Miss Dora?"

Sage nearly tore the page in half. She felt the blood drain from her face. "Not her, too. Fifty years ago?" Then she remembered the gash and crimson drip from the woman's hair. Everyone at the manor was *dead*?

* * *

Sage trampled through the high grass, something chasing behind her. Heavy footsteps. She turned to look but saw nothing. The sky grew darker, the manor the only thing in view, though a long distance away. Her breath huffing, she kept running. Her neck prickled, a presence closing in on her. The stink of rancid meat.

She ran faster. Sharp objects, like needles, swept across her shoulder. She cried out, grasped her shoulder then turned. A bulky shadow loomed over her.

"Go, get away from me!" she yelled. Her shoulder felt damp, and it stung. She looked at her hand; a warm dark liquid covered it. Blood? The sky dimmed further and color was hard to see.

Heart in her throat, she backed away from the shadow. She thought she heard a sneering laugh. Suddenly, she tripped over something solid and hard. She landed in the grass, bristling, and cold.

A head! A woman's stone head. That's what tripped her. Was it the head from the fountain? Half buried in the dirt, its mouth gaped open, as if to scream. Sage stared up. The shadow had vanished.

She jerked upright with a gasp, but she was in bed, in her own room. She touched her shoulder; no pain. She bunched her sheets in her fists. A dream, a horrible dream. Was the creature trying to frighten her off?

Chapter 25

Sage promised her mother they were heading to town and not the manor. "First, I want to tell you what I dreamed last night," she said once they'd left their house and yard. If she got it out in the open, she might not feel so disturbed.

"Do you think it was the shapeshifter?" Patrick asked when she finished. He looked skeptical. "Was it trying to kill you?"

"Sounds scary. And it scratched you?" Nate glanced at her shoulder.

"It might be the shapeshifter. It was just a shadow, and very scary." Sage pressed on her shoulder, remembering the claw-like sting. She suppressed a quiver. But now the bulky shadow made her angry. She wanted to destroy it—if she could. "Then tripping over the fountain's head."

"We should search for that in the area around the manor." Patrick walked faster as they left Cliff Street for Nahant Road.

Nate lagged behind.

"Have you changed your mind about going?" Sage asked, slowing with him. "I won't mind if—"

"No. I wanted to ask you." His large eyes searched hers. "Do you think Mom and

Dad will stay together, not like Patrick's parents?"

"Oh, has this been bothering you?" Sage slowed even more and kept in step with him. "It looks like they've made up and will be fine. Really. Mom and Dad told me so."

"Good. I heard some of what you said to Dad at the Rock Temple" He gave her a small smile. "But I feel bad for Aunt Theresa. And Patrick."

"So do I." She hugged her brother, and he didn't resist. "We can talk again anytime, but let's catch up to him."

The humidity was thick today, the ocean glittering in the sunlight. A Beach Plum on the far side of the road wavered in a slight breeze.

"Our parents look happier now," Nate said, increasing his stride.

"Much happier." Sage smiled. "Patrick, wait up!"

Two dune buggies zoomed by, with loud and laughing tourists, probably headed for the causeway and Long Beach with its narrow strip of dunes. Sage fanned away the stink of diesel.

When they reached the strip of shops, she said, "Okay, you two behave in the shop. No witch jokes."

"I'm a changed person." Patrick grinned briefly, then pumped his arms as they walked. Maybe he *would* try. "Your dream was awesome, but I still can't believe that story about Miss Dora dying in a car crash. How can it be the same Dora Brubaker?"

"That's the problem. At the manor, you never know who is who." Sage's brain buzzed with the decisions she had to make, how much to admit to the boys. And Miss Dora had always seemed an odd person. Sage had suspected she might be a ghost.

"We talked to her, and she talked to us, like normal people." Nate hurried to keep up. "Does that mean we speak to ghosts, too?"

"There's different...layers of ghosts, I guess." Sage tried to form it clearly—her bizarre life. Grandma Esther seemed on a deeper layer, one further from the present world. Not that Sage was a Ghost Expert.

"What about the butler, Huntley? Is he real or a ghost?" Patrick scuffed his sneakers through the dirt beside the road.

"If I tell you, you must keep it secret. And don't say anything to Mr. Huntley." Sage brushed her hair from her face. "The butler could be a ghost." She wasn't ready to confess he was the love their Grandma Esther had shot. She selfishly liked the truth kept between her and Huntley. "And there's something more. You'll find out today. It has to do with my dream, too."

"Are we going to let Mom meet Miss Dora?" Nate asked.

"If she insists, what can we do?" Sage cringed at that idea. A tea party with two ghosts. Who else might show up? Count

Dracula? "If she hadn't been so busy with her work schedule, Mom would have asked sooner, I'm sure."

"What *more* do you mean? Tell us now," Patrick said in a non-demanding voice, as if he struggled to chill.

"No, you'll have to wait." Sage stopped when they reached Mrs. Crippin's shop. She took a very deep breath and opened the door. The bell tinkled. She entered the coolness of the shop, the boys behind her. The smell of spices and flowers sweetened the air.

After a rustling in the back, Mrs. Crippin stepped up to the counter. Her burgundy-colored hair was tied in a messy knot atop her head. "Oh, three young people grace me with their presence. How intriguing." She smiled, but her eyes held a sharp interest.

"You know my brother Nate, and my cousin Patrick," Sage said.

"Of course. Young Nate, you've grown taller. And Patrick, Theresa's son. Such a handsome young man. How is your mother?" Her large hoop earrings swung above the shoulders of her purple caftan. "You moved to Connecticut, how do you like it?"

"I like my school." Patrick stared around the shop, hands behind his back. "My mom's okay. Considering."

"There's so much cool stuff in here." Nate touched a crystal on a low shelf, then looked to see if his sister watched. She did.

"I wondered if you...had time to search into what we talked about?" Sage bit down on her lip as she moved close to the counter. Was she too hopeful?

Mrs. Crippin cocked her head, her topknot wagging. "I researched into the lore of the area, which I already knew much about, and of Lakeluster House. The ancient mysteries. This island is millions of years old." She glanced at the boys. "Are they part of this?"

"Yes, if they can both keep secrets." Sage turned to them. Patrick nodded with a frown. Nate nodded enthusiastically.

"Very well. Though I'm reluctant." Mrs. Crippin dug around under the counter. "According to my..." She stared at the front door. "Patrick, please flip the sign to Closed. We must not be disturbed."

He did so. He and Nate moved to stand on each side of Sage.

"If my dear Walter knew of this escapade, and often the 'other' side knows everything, he'd caution me. I miss him dreadfully, but we don't need to discuss that." The woman pulled out a tiny bottle with a stopper. "This mixture, and I can't tell you the ingredients, I found in an old book of spells. The book was printed in Salem back in the seventeenth century. My daughter works there, especially during

Halloween. We're from a long line of Charmers." She tapped a shiny red nail on the bottle's top. "It said, in the English of an earlier time, to slow the beast, you must sprinkle the liquid in its eyes."

Sage held her breath. They *would* have to get very close. "Isn't there an easier way? Poison left in food near where it creeps around?"

"What are we talking about?" Nate's voice had risen. "What's this beast?"

"Nate, I didn't want to tell you." Sage clasped his arm. "But you want to be included. There's a terrible creature at the manor. I'm pretty sure it's what killed Mr. Saunders."

"The shapeshifter? Your dream. That shadow was the beast?" Patrick asked. "If any of this is real. Okay, it could be real." He didn't sound mocking, only a little leery. "Wouldn't a gun be better?"

"I'd rather you stayed home," Sage said to her brother.

"No. I'll be strong." Nate puffed out his cheeks. "Will it hurt us?"

"It could hurt us." Sage turned to Mrs. Crippin. "Does the potion kill the creature?"

"Sorry, it won't. For that, after you've calmed it down—" She leaned close, her eyes almost cat-like beneath her thick false eyelashes. "This is the difficult part. You have to shove a golden spike down its throat."

"A golden spike?" Sage stared at the woman, her heart jumping. "Like a stake for a vampire?"

"Can we get help to kill it?" Nate asked, eyes darting from the woman to Sage.

"A wizard maybe?" Patrick's smile was amused, as if it was all a game. Or he hid his wariness. "Just zap it away."

"Be serious. Where can we get a gold spike?" Sage felt dizzy, half ready to run from this. But she couldn't. She'd made some unspoken promise. More information from Bella might be the key. If she ever saw the girl again.

"A terrifying creature," Nate muttered. "Hard to believe—"

"I want to believe." Patrick shook his head, his cheeks aflame. "Is it like that thing you made in your bedroom? Do we really get to kill something? This could be...exciting."

"It won't be exciting." Sage strained to steady her own panic. "Other ghosts are trapped in the house. And the beast could kill another innocent person, like Mr. Saunders."

"I'm afraid that's true." Mrs. Crippin sighed, earrings swinging. "The creature might be related to a Chepi. A demon that plays painful tricks, as told of by the Wampanoag Tribe, who first occupied Massachusetts. You children have quite the task before you. Are you certain you want to do this?"

Murder is certainly painful, and dangerous, Sage fumed.

"Where do we find this spike?" Could Sage trust what the woman said? She clamped her hands on the counter.

"That I don't know. But the manor holds many secrets. I've done what I can." Mrs. Crippin watched them, frowning. "It will be risky. I would advise against such an endeavor, but you seem to have been chosen. You have a blood connection, deeper than you think. Still, find an adult to assist."

Why Sage was chosen, she still wasn't sure. But a deeper blood connection? Maybe Huntley could advise her. And Bella once asked for her help. She snatched the bottle. "I know it's hazardous, yet I have to do something."

The woman pulled a packet from under the counter. "This is filled with oregano. It protects you from evil. Do I need to make two more?"

"I hope my brother won't go." Sage glanced at him. Her nerves tripped along her spine. She needed Patrick, probably, for his bullish strength, plus he might tell her parents what was going on if she didn't include him. But she still felt protective of Nate.

"This is like a horror movie." Nate held his fists up. "But I want to come."

"I'm definitely going. Mainly, to protect my cousins." Patrick squared his shoulders. "I'm the oldest one. And the smartest."

"How do I pay for the potion?" Sage hid her doubts and fears, scrunching them tight inside her.

"Can't you just make it disappear?" Patrick raised his eyebrows at Mrs. Crippin. He obviously was still skeptical.

"Nothing is that simple." Mrs. Crippin studied them again. "You must keep this a secret. Those old biddies in the Nahant Historical Society already tried to run me out of town, years ago, for *odd* practices. Some people have no imagination or don't understand the supernatural." She reached across the counter and placed her hand on Sage's head and whispered words Sage couldn't understand. "There, a spell to give you a chance at success. The potion is my gift."

Sage needed more than 'a chance'. She stuffed the oregano pouch in her bra and couldn't deny this challenge stimulated her—coated with dread—despite what she'd said to Patrick.

Chapter 26

After breakfast the next day, Sage waited until her mom was busy at her computer, before she slipped out the back door with Patrick and Nate behind her. The morning air held a hint of humidity as they hurried down the street toward the woods.

Entering the coolness of the trees, Sage said, "Dad had to go to Salem to teach a summer class. Their professor had his appendix removed."

"You trust Uncle Ron, I guess." Patrick shoved his thumbs in his pants pockets.

"Of course. We all do." She smiled at Nate and wished Patrick hadn't brought that up about her dad's affair. She did trust him now. As she walked, inhaling the forest smells, plus the herb nestled in her bra, her head filled with what they might face at the manor. A ghostly Miss Dora. The creature in the attic. Nothing real could be counted on. The unknown threatened to swallow her up.

"Do you know how we're going to do this?" Patrick asked. "I know I'll believe it when I see the thing. We should call it ChepiTwo."

"I've no plan yet." Sage hoped to talk to Bella and Huntley. She kicked aside pebbles with her boots. Would this be a grand battle, or would they end up as monster food? *Gross!* She must believe they could destroy the creature. But would the boys even *see* it, since these horrors usually showed themselves only to her? "I want you to protect Nate."

"Don't leave me out. I'm right here." Nate slapped a pine branch.

"Just stick by Patrick," she replied. How she wished he had stayed home.

An animal rustled through the brush.

"It might be a coyote." Sage peered through the trees. "They attack cats and dogs. People carry baseball bats when they walk their pets."

Footsteps sounded behind them.

"That's not a coyote," Nate said. He turned, walking backwards.

"No, it's me." Their mom stalked towards them in white linen pants and white sneakers. Her face was determined, her thick, dark hair bouncing on the shoulders of her green blouse.

"Hi, Aunt Jenny. We're out for fresh air," Patrick said, his smile broad.

"And headed straight for the manor." Jenny halted in front of them as the three stopped walking. "You snuck out and thought I wouldn't notice; but I was paying attention."

"We're going to visit." Sage smiled. But desperation surged inside her. "If that's okay."

"Well, you can include me on your visit. It's about time." Jenny resumed walking down the path. "I've been negligent in coming out here."

"They might not care for a stranger." Sage followed, her gut tightening. "They may not let us in the house." How could she ask for golden spikes with her mom there?

"We'll find out, won't we." Jenny kept up a brisk pace. "I'm your mother and I intend to know more about these people you spend so much time with. I should have done this weeks ago."

"You might not want—" Nate cut off when Patrick poked his shoulder.

"You're welcome to join us," Patrick said, his theatrical words grating on Sage's nerves. "A big tea party."

"But Miss Dora is sometimes resting. She's an odd person. But sweet." Sage fumbled for excuses. *And everyone there is dead!*

They reached the edge of the forest, the manor before them.

After crossing the clearing, Sage mounted the steps and knocked on the front door. She felt the bottle of potion in her jeans pocket. This was going so wrong. The others joined her.

The door opened. Huntley stood there, actually wearing a sharp navy-blue jacket, as if he expected them. He smiled, his gaze kind. "Am I to understand this is your mother?"

Sage gulped and forced a smile. "Yes, this is Mrs. Jenny Emery, Nate and mine's mother." She turned to her mom. "Mom, this is Mr. Huntley. Miss Dora's butler."

"I'm pleased to meet you. I love your English accent." Jenny stepped forward, eyes sparkling, and held out her hand. "I'm sorry to intrude on such short notice. I'd like to meet Miss Dora Brubaker."

"Indeed. She'll be overjoyed to have company." Huntly squeezed her hand and bowed slightly. "Please come in."

Sage entered with the rest, caught by the scent of lemon furniture polish. The house looked immaculate, with fresh flowers in vases on a buffet. Wooden floors shone and the chandelier glistened, adorned with several lit candles. Even the wallpaper looked more colorful. What a change.

Nate stared around, his eyes wide in wonder.

Patrick exchanged a look of surprise with Sage.

"This is quite grand," Jenny said. "You've fixed the house up nicely."

Huntley bowed again. "I'll tell Miss Dora that you're here." He left them.

"Did you ever come here as a kid?" Sage asked her mom, unsure how to take this transformation. The ghosts aways surprised her.

"My parents, your grandparents, told me to stay away from this decrepit place. But I did come out here a few times with your Aunt

Theresa. We played in the woods, though never went inside the house. We were scared off by rumors it was haunted." Jenny pressed Sage's shoulder. "I wasn't as brave as you."

"I was the bold one," Patrick declared. He obviously couldn't resist boasting. "I insisted we come into the house. I slayed it."

Sage smirked. "You're right, you were the brave one."

"I get more dope every day," Nate said, chin high.

"Don't be careless trying to be daring," Jenny warned. She hugged Nate. "You aren't adults yet."

Huntley returned. "Please, follow me. You can join Miss Dora for morning tea."

Sage gaped at the small sitting room. It no longer looked shabby, but bright and polished. More vases of fresh flowers. The table near the kitchen was covered with a pale pink linen cloth, lace at the edges. She dared to look at Huntley, and he raised one eyebrow, his eyes glistening with mischief.

Miss Dora rose from her chair, her smile welcoming. This woman Sage was now pretty sure was a ghost.

"Please, join me, Mrs. Emery. I'm honored by your visit." Miss Dora wore an attractive pink dress with tiny lavender flowers, her gray hair in softer curls about her round face, as if she too expected their company.

Huntley pulled out a chair at the table's other end. Jenny thanked him and sat. "I've been meaning to visit you, Miss Brubaker. Excuse my tardiness in coming. Welcome home. Sage tells me you were born here."

"I was. And lived here until I was about three. Then my mother took me to England," Miss Dora said. "We visited here later, for a few summers. It is good to be home."

"I understand. My family has lived in Nahant for generations. Our house was built in the eighteenth century, supposedly owned by a cunning woman." Jenny laughed. "A kinder word for witch."

Huntley pulled out a chair to Jenny's left and looked at Sage. She fought the urge to run upstairs and search for Bella. Instead, she sat. "Thank you."

The boys took chairs opposite each other, trying not to look at one another.

"Huntley, you may serve us." Miss Dora raised a hand.

"I hope we're not intruding. You needn't go to any trouble." Jenny spread a napkin on her lap.

"Nonsense. You are most welcome. My stepfather, since my parents divorced, shameful to say, always said make your guests comfortable." Miss Dora squinted; she wore no glasses today.

"Polite company is always appreciated." Huntley looked briefly at Patrick.

Sage sat rigid in her chair as the butler poured tea into delicate cups. He placed a sugar bowl, a small pitcher of milk, then a plate of tiny cakes on the table.

"Please, enjoy the *petit fours*." Miss Dora nodded toward the little cakes.

Nate and Patrick both reached for one. Huntley waved them away and slipped a silver serving tool under a cake. He served Miss Dora, Jenny, and Sage. Then he gave cakes to the boys.

Sage had little appetite. This was all too normal, yet overly perfect—a staged event—and it put her on edge.

"The cake is delicious," her mom said after tasting a bite. "Thank you. Now, what do you and the kids like to discuss when they visit?"

"The new garden," Sage blurted. She hurriedly took a bite of cake, the chocolate icing icky sweet.

"Your daughter is interested in the manor history," Huntley said with a brief smile. "She's learned an enormous amount."

That's an understatement, Sage tried not to say. "I have learned lots."

"We're all interested in the history." Patrick grinned, then finished his cake. "The spooky stuff, too."

Nate nodded, wiping icing from his mouth with a cloth napkin. "The spooky stuff is fun and...interesting."

Sage sagged with relief he didn't say 'scary'.

"The children are fascinated by this grand old house." Miss Dora sipped her tea. "I certainly can't blame them. I found it a wonderland as a child."

Sage noticed the lion statues on the cabinet. Did one actually narrow its eyes? She slopped milk into her tea.

"And the story of my Great Grandmother Esther, who was a housekeeper here." Jenny drank from her cup as she scanned all three of them. "Sage says she solved the mystery."

"Mom, we don't need to talk about that." Sage squirmed in the chair. She glanced at Huntley in apology.

"I'll prepare more tea. Excuse me." Huntley's gaze turned painful. He picked up the pot and entered the kitchen.

"The mystery?" Miss Dora tilted her head. A red gash appeared on one side, her hair matted, like in a car wreck. Then it changed back. "Oh, the rumor that a servant was murdered here. And your ancestor might be involved."

If she's dead, too, she must know everything. Especially since Huntley is her butler. These thoughts bounced around in Sage's head, along with the glimpse of the gash. This matched what she'd seen before on Miss Dora's head. She chewed the inside of her cheek, then remembered she'd broken that habit.

Sage stood. She needed to speak to Huntley alone about spikes and flinging potion into a beast's eyes. Would he know? "I'll go help him."

"Sit down, please, young lady. Huntley needs no help." Miss Dora sounded sharper than she'd ever heard before.

"Apparently my relative is guilty, so my daughter stated." Jenny gave Sage and Miss Dora a curious look. "This tale has hung over us for so long. I was hoping for the opposite."

"It seems true. Guilty." Sage sat and picked up her teacup, the tea sloshing. She felt a twinge of sorrow for Huntley's brutal death.

"She won't give us all the details either," Patrick said, though kept his voice light. He was really trying to be nicer.

"What is the spooky stuff that you said was fun?" Jenny gazed at Nate, then Patrick. "Have you gone upstairs?"

"The old house is full of creaks and groans, a few dark corners, perhaps a hidden passage, nothing more." Miss Dora sounded sweet again. "Yes, the children have gone upstairs with Huntley."

"There's also a basement with torture tools," Nate said, his gaze intense.

"Yeah, real dangerous and creepy things," Patrick agreed with a wink. "Would you like to see them, Aunt Jenny?"

"No, she wouldn't." Sage glared at him, then softened it with a brittle smile.

"Oh, don't be silly, young gentlemen." Miss Dora laughed, almost a girlish giggle. "As if we'd have something so terrible here."

"They've enjoyed these visits. But I'd like the children to participate in the town's summer activities." Would her mom insist they no longer visit?

Sage took another bite of cake, but it tasted dry and stale in her mouth.

"I can understand that." Miss Dora continued to smile, her eyes unfocused. "Children should be children. Play while you can. Tomorrow isn't promised."

Footsteps overhead, like last time at tea. Sage tightened her muscles. Was it Bella?

Huntley returned with the teapot. "Does anyone need anything else?" His pointed stare pierced Sage. *We need Miss Emery here*, he seemed to declare. The voice in her head again.

The room appeared to lean to the left, and Sage felt a strange floating sensation. She clutched her chair edges with her fingers. Everyone else at the table had stilled—frozen in place. Shadows deepened in the room's corners as if collapsing in on her. One of the lion statues raised a paw and showed its teeth. Her body shuddered.

Huntley indicated for Sage to look behind her. She turned in her chair. Her heart lifted for a second. Bella stood there, beckoning, her little face bruised, her apron dripping with mud.

Chapter 27

Sage rose on unsteady feet. No one at the table moved. She approached Bella, about to ask if she was okay. No, she *wasn't*; she was dead. She smelled of mud and pond scum.

"I'm so sorry about what happened at the pond." Sage wanted to cup the child's bruised cheeks.

"An evil man, but it's done. We shouldn't weep over what cannot be changed." Bella headed for the stairs, her reddish braids bouncing off her back, her apron leaving drips on the floor.

"I wish I could have been there and protected you." A silly wish. They both could have been murdered. Sage followed her to the third floor. "Bella, did this creature in the attic kill Mr. Saunders?"

"It did. The beast rarely leaves the house, but that time it crawled out to hang the body. Your teacher was too persistent in his questions." Bella shook her head. "A horrible incident. The more evil in this house, the worse the creature became."

Sage blew out a frustrated breath, her pulse jumping. She remembered what Mrs. Crippin had said. "Why was I chosen to...to get rid of it?"

Bella turned, her face now clear, the mud dried. "You're attached to this house. Not only through your Grandmother Esther's act, but you're related to me, through my mother's family. Her great aunt had married a Brubaker, that's our connection to Lakeluster."

"How could that be?" Then Sage was also related by marriage to the Brubakers? An eerie notion. "We would have known."

"There was a base-born child. A child out of wedlock, so no one in this family claimed it. No one spoke of such things back in the early 1900s. Your father comes from that person." Bella smiled, but briefly. "We're distant cousins."

"I'm glad we're related." Sage filled with a mixture of pity and confusion. She ached to hug the child. Here was the blood connection Mrs. Crippin mentioned. Yet why choose a young girl to destroy a beast? She touched the potion bottle in her pocket again, then glanced up at the trapdoor.

"There isn't much time," Bella said. "It's restless and wants to roam farther. It fights the sin of Sloth. I brought you up here to hear the desperation. To understand."

Clicks and pacing sounded from the attic. A low growl.

"Oh no." Sage fisted her hands. This was happening too fast. She had to grab every ounce of courage to fulfill...what? A destiny? "Do you know where I can find a golden spike?" Her question came out a jittery whisper.

A commotion on the stairs and the boys appeared, Patrick frowning. "You snuck off from us. You promised you wouldn't."

"Where is Mom?" Sage looked at her brother in alarm.

Huntley walked toward them. "Your mum had a lively talk with Miss Dora, then I saw her out the door. A charming woman."

"She didn't notice I was missing?" Sage searched the butler's face for teasing.

"*We* didn't notice until Mom left." Nate crossed his arms, eyebrows lowered. "How'd you do it?"

Huntley patted Nate's shoulder, then smiled at her. "Everything is fine, Miss Emery. It was handled. Your mum left safely."

Some ghost magic? The back of Sage's neck prickled. "I hope Mom was satisfied and won't forbid us visiting."

"Aunt Jenny was good. So, what's the plan now?" Patrick looked up, a glint in his eye, though his fingers clenched and unclenched. "Do we go into the attic after ChepiTwo?"

"Don't be so anxious," Huntley warned. "More arrangements must be put in order."

"Did you see..." Sage turned, but Bella was no longer there. Sage huffed. Would she come back?

"We still need a spike." Nate glanced at Huntley. "How much does he know?" he whispered to Sage.

"I think he knows, and has always known, everything." Sage said it softly, hiding her exasperation.

Huntley made a slight nod.

"Why doesn't he kill the beast?" Patrick asked with a flip of his hand. "Why we outsiders? Not that I don't want to."

"Because we need a warm-blooded, blood-connected person for that." Huntley pinned Patrick with a steely eye, one eyebrow raised.

But you're sacrificing me! She scrubbed that thought away.

Now the butler watched her with concern in his gaze.

"Are you really a ghost?" Nate backed up a step. "I can't see through you."

"Do something ghostly," Patrick urged. "Like floating."

"Stop it." Sage rippled with the nerves building up inside her. "Show respect. We need to help each other." She'd rather Huntley acted the non-ghostly way he usually did. It kept her grounded.

"How are we blood connected?" Patrick asked. "Though the weird witch said the same."

"Ignore them." Sage faced Huntley, nudging the boys aside as she kept the desperation from her voice. "Do you know where I can find a golden spike?"

"Try the library. There are interesting items there." At a scratching overhead, Huntley stared up. Both boys did the same. The scratching grew more intense, as if it might claw through the ceiling. Sage fought a tremor as icy cold slit through her veins.

* * *

In the library, Sage studied everything, the bookshelves, the fireplace mantel, the window. "A spike could be hidden anywhere."

Patrick searched the desk and then the mantel. He pushed on the crest, but no secret passage opened up. Nate pulled out and pushed in books. A musty smell rose into the air.

Patrick checked the table where the handcuffs were. They were no longer there. "You never told me; how are we blood related to this place?"

"You're not. My dad is descended from a born-on-the-side person from the early 1900s." Sage stared at the ceiling. Could a spike be imbedded up there?

"What's born on the side?" Nate dropped a book and quickly picked it up.

"The girl I speak to, yes she's a ghost, Bella, she told me. One of her mother's family had a child but wasn't married." Sage examined the surbases; anything gold?

"Back then, many years ago, it was a big shock."

"I know you've mentioned her. You've been talking with another ghost all this time." Patrick accused, brow furrowed. "More secrets."

"You haven't said much about her," Nate said. "Yeah, more secrets."

Sage pushed on panels around the room. Were any hollow? The lions carved in the mantel flicked a glance at her. She moved away. "She's a child ghost. I could hardly believe it myself."

"Was she murdered?" Nate asked, mouth pursed.

"Yes. At only ten. Bella saw Harrison Brubaker poison his first wife." Sage felt the sadness again, but it switched to anger at such cruelty.

"Are you telling us a story?" Patrick knocked hard on all the panels around the fireplace. "We might as well be lost in *Stranger Things*. Or *The Squid Game*."

"How was she killed?" Nate sounded nervous now. He went to the window, pushing on the curtains that Sage had already pushed aside.

She peeled up the rug near the desk. Would there be a hidden compartment? *What if we can't find it?* "Brubaker let her fall into the pond and watched her drown."

Patrick ran his fingers over every nook and cranny. "Ominous. But we'd better get used to ominous. That scratching noise was freakin' chilling."

At least they had all heard the noise this time. Sage peeled back the rug on the desk's other side, breathing in spurts. "We need a ladder to check those higher bookshelves." She looked up. The books on the top shelf appeared to rearrange themselves with disturbing sounds of leather on leather. The boys seemed unaware.

Something slid out from the bookcase. A short, bald man with large, thick-lensed glasses and a purple birthmark on one temple. He grinned at Sage, his teeth yellow and crooked. He resembled her middle school librarian, except that guy had better teeth. "Can I help you find something, Miss Emery?"

"Noooo!" but the shout stayed trapped in her throat. "You're trying to trick me."

"I can be quite helpful if you'll allow it." He raised his stubby fingers, a bit of drool escaping his mouth.

"You're part of the evil, I can see it." Sage held her body still as she crouched. Her pulse drummed in her ears. This had to be the creature, shifting in shape. "Get away from me. I'm not ready for you."

"You won't stop me, little girl. I'm too powerful now." He winked, his eyes cold and empty. His mouth opened wide, a gaping hole she might fall into among the stench of foul breath.

Sage swallowed hard, fingers tight on the carpet, but she kept her gaze steady. "You don't scare me." A lie.

After a nasty laugh, it rippled from head to toe, then slinked back between the books.

She hopped up, stumbling on her feet. Her body flinched, like ants crawled all over her. She had to quit asking herself how she was going to do any of this. It was a frightening, fantasy-horror land she must master. She would stop it!

She turned toward the window where Nate still stood, and something glinted at the top, a sparkling bar. "Do you see that, Nate?"

Nate stared up. "Yes! It's the curtain rod."

Sage joined him. So did Patrick. The rod was a gold color. Patrick dragged over the desk chair, climbed up, and unhooked the two curtain panels. They slid in a heap to the floor. He lifted the rod from its brackets.

He jumped down with it. "Look. It's sharp on one end."

Sage sucked in her breath. She slowly reached out and touched the smooth metal. "This must be the spike." There was no turning back now.

Chapter 28

With Patrick holding the spike, sharp end up, the three of them returned to the third floor. Huntley awaited them.

"Congratulations. You found the spike." Huntley's tone subdued, he eyed it with a frown, as if he regretted this entire operation.

"I found it," Nate said, his lower lip jutting out. "I'm good at finding things."

Sage decided not to mention she'd pointed it out. "What do you know about this creature?" she asked the butler, hoping he had a better solution.

"We're all full of some type of sin. Here, the ugliness tapped into something malevolent." Huntley spoke low. "A menace burrowed in the ground long before the manor was built."

"Like from Indian times?" Patrick lifted the spike. "Same as that witch, Mrs. Crippin said."

"It's native American, not Indian," Sage reminded, then wondered why bother.

"The sins took an animal form, feeding off the deviant happenings in this house. When the basement was dug out, that disturbed the sleeping demons, according to the indigenous people who once lived on

Nahant. Some of the tribes came back to protest Mr. Brubaker's greed. And ruthless deeds. He spent his money on his own luxury and never put anything back into Nahant or its people." Huntley's voice turned sad. "And I added to the sins, along with your Grandmother Esther."

"How did you add to it?" Patrick narrowed his eyes.

"I didn't tell them." Sage held up her hands, unnerved by all of it. "Don't be upset, Patrick. I kept more secrets."

"I'm the one your Grandmother Esther shot." Huntley made a mocking bow. "Don't blame your sister."

"Whaaat?" Nate's mouth dropped open.

"How's that possible?" Patrick thumped the spike on the floor. "Oh, in this house I guess it could be. You are a ghost. For real? She killed you?"

"I've seen Grandmother Esther many times. She rarely speaks to me." Sage tensed, remembering the shooting, the blood.

"How long have you known about him being part of the murder?" Patrick scowled at her, the spike raised.

"What else do you know?" Nate asked, his voice angry.

"Please, let's figure out what we're going to do." Sage turned to Huntley. "How do we get the beast to come out?" She tugged the tiny bottle from her pocket. "I'm supposed to sprinkle this potion in its eyes."

"I would advise you to perform that from a distance. You don't wish to be hurt." Huntley looked them over, his gaze troubled. "You don't have to attempt this. It's a perilous act."

"But we do. I *must*." Sage was chosen, no matter her wishes. Her heart pinched. "From a distance... A squirt gun. That's what I need."

"I have one at home. I could go get it." Nate shifted on his feet. "It's in my closet, on the top shelf."

"I'll get it." Patrick handed the spike to Sage. "Aunt Jenny might make you stay home."

"I wish she would," Sage muttered under her breath as she gripped the weapon. Could she ram this down the creature's maw? Bile gurgled in her own throat. "Hurry."

"Don't do anything until I get back." Patrick dashed for the stairs.

The air seemed to thicken. The stained glass at the hall's far end rearranged its design again. Letters formed the word: Persevere.

Sage stared harder. She knew that meant *keep trying*. Shadows deepened, darkening around Nate and Huntley like a veil.

Her throat tightening, she reached to grab her brother, to keep him close. But Bella was suddenly beside her.

"To bring out the creature, if it doesn't want to show itself," Bella looked around, "you must confer with the spirit of a Wampanoag shaman."

"Where would I find one of those?" Sage bristled with frustration. There were too many ghosts here already. "Do we really need this Chepi thing destroyed? It can't be tamed?"

"You don't want another horrible death like Mr. Saunders, do you?" Bella bunched her apron in her hands.

"No. Never." Sage slumped her shoulders, then straightened them. She was the chosen one and had to be brave in this fractured fairy tale. Here was the thrill she sought. "I shouldn't have even asked."

"I'll find the shaman for you. I've learned to be sturdy and clever since my drowning." Bella turned and evaporated into the wall.

Thumping on the stairs. Patrick appeared, his face red and sweaty. How had he returned so fast? More confusing dimensions.

"I've got it." He held up the squirt gun, his breathing strained. "Aunt Jenny asked what I was doing. I said we're at the public pool, playing a game."

Nate stepped from the shadows. Sage didn't see Huntley. Somehow, his presence had comforted her.

"Are you okay?" She touched her brother's cheek.

"Why wouldn't I be?" Nate shuffled aside.

"What do we do now? Call 'hey, kitty, kitty'?" Patrick handed the squirt gun to Nate and tried to take the spike from Sage.

"I'm keeping this. It's my job to shove it down ChepiTwo's throat." Sage clutched the stake tighter. Maybe they could entice the beast out if Bella didn't return. She gave Nate the potion. "Fill the squirt gun."

A movement to her right made her turn. A semi-transparent man took shape. His wizened face was framed by an array of feathers, like a starburst on gray hair. He wore a wide headband and a long buckskin cloak.

He raised his arms. "You have brought this evil on yourselves for stealing sacred land. Now we must prepare. Step back, children."

"What's here? Something else is here." Patrick gazed around. "I hear faint words."

Sage dragged her brother to her. "Patrick, come near us. No arguing."

"What's happening?" Patrick followed. "Is there another ghost?"

"Is the monster coming out?" Nate's eyes flitted back and forth.

"Just wait, please," Sage urged.

The shaman started chanting. The air turned frigid, almost foggy.

Sage's head throbbed, her breath sharp. The chants sent chills up her spine.

The trapdoor creaked open. All three children groaned.

A long, hairy arm with spiky claws swiped down from the opening. A nasty, meaty stink filled the air. The shaman stepped closer. Beastly talons sliced through his raised arm. The arm detached, then reattached.

"Ugh! I think I see an Indian." Patrick sounded on the verge of fear. "Did you see that arm, those claws?"

"Hush." Sage bit her cheek, the spike gripped in one hand, her brother's shoulder in the other. Here it came, the monster of sins.

"Oww!" Nate pulled away from her, rubbing his shoulder.

The shaman swept his arms in an arc, lowering his head, feathers swaying. The ceiling seemed to close in, throwing murky shadows. Shadows with substance that crept around them.

A face on a long neck appeared from the opening. An ugly face that resembled the creature Sage created in her room. Its mouth gaping, ChepiTwo snarled. The walls on both sides shook.

The shaman vanished in a shaft of light.

Patrick stumbled back. Sage sucked down a shriek and pushed Nate back.

"I need to shoot in its eyes," Nate insisted, hugging the squirt gun to his chest. "You do see it? We all see it."

The beast crawled from the attic, lithe, like a cat. Saliva dripped from its jaws.

"Give me the squirt gun," Patrick demanded.

Ape-like legs spread, blood-shot eyes focused on them, ChepiTwo wrinkled up its lips, showing sharp fangs.

"I can do it!" Nate's arm quivered as he moved forward and pointed the gun. The beast swiped the gun from his hand, sending it clattering across the floor.

"Nooo." Blood formed on Nate's hand. Sage moaned, her cheek stinging.

The beast advanced, the knobs on its head wriggling. ChepiTwo rose on its hind legs, roaring, claws scratching at the air above their heads. Her brother shrank down.

Sage snatched Nate's collar and shoved him behind her. She backed up several steps as she jolted. Should they run? No, she *couldn't*. They needed that gun!

"Sheet, bro!" Patrick yelled. The beast swiped at him. He ducked.

Sage held her breath and stepped to its left, to retrieve the gun.

"Your sins are finished!" Huntley now stood to the creature's right.

The beast turned its head. Patrick scooted low along the floor, pushing in front of her, and grabbed the squirt gun. He scrambled back.

"You need to set us free," Bella called, appearing at the wall.

"Squirt it!" Sage ordered, the spike pointed at the monster. "Hurry up!"

ChepiTwo loomed over them, his stink overpowering. Sage's legs almost buckled beneath her. It snatched out a paw and grabbed her hair, dragging her toward it. Saliva dripped on her face, a sizzling, damp stench. She flinched. Was she done for?

Nate wadded the back of her blouse and bra strap in his hands, pulling. "I got you."

She yelled and yanked back her head, the pain sharp. Terror surged through her. "Squirt now!"

Patrick jabbed the gun forward and squirted the liquid, but splattered its nose. The creature growled and released her, then swiped at Patrick's arm. Her cousin jerked, blood dripping from his arm. Then he squirted again. This time he hit the beast in the eyes. ChepiTwo howled, rubbing at its eyes.

"I did it. I splashed it." Patrick raised his hands, the blood spreading to his shirt sleeve. "Ouch! But I'm the man."

"Get away from that thing!" Sage wrenched him by the shoulder with her as she moved back. She tucked his arm to his shirt front to slow the blood, her scalp smarting. "Protect Nate."

"I could have done it." Nate wiped the blood from his hand.

The beast rocked back and forth, howling like a wolf. Then it changed its shape, into a man. Sage's father.

"Don't believe its tricks," Huntley warned. "You must spike it, Miss Emery."

"I will!" She positioned the spike, which now felt so heavy she could hardly hold it.

"Don't hurt me, dear," her fake-father pleaded. "I love you. Everything will be all right."

"You aren't my dad." Sage cringed, the voice so Dad-like. She thought of Mr. Saunders instead. An innocent man only doing research. Skinned to the bone. She crept closer.

Her fake-dad changed, reforming, and Grandma Esther appeared. "Please, honey, you cannot injure us. It's partly my fault, continuing the sins."

A gust of wind swirled around Sage, almost knocking her over. The spike wobbled in her hands.

"That is not Essie!" Huntley shouted, though hurt flashed in his eyes.

"How could you doubt me, Jacob?" Her pretend two-greats grandma looked so sweet, so innocent. "I'm sorry for what I did to you."

"You are not my grandmother!" Sage cried, her wrists in pain from holding the weapon. "Show us what you really are."

"Stop hiding!" Bella cried.

Pretend-grandma opened her mouth, wide and red; fangs appeared, saliva dribbled. It transformed again, back into the hairy animal. But ChepiTwo's front legs moved slowly, and it made feeble swipes with its paws.

"Do it, do it!" Patrick urged, clutching his arm. Blood seeped through his fingers. "If you can't, I will."

"Be careful," Nate squeaked.

"You can destroy it," Huntley said. "You must. Here's your destiny."

Sage hefted the spike, her heart galloping in her chest. The beast snarled, but not so loudly. It kept rubbing at now red, infected eyes.

In a burst of anger, the monster lashed out its tongue, burning a hole in the wall. Sage felt the heat on her face and smelled her hair singe. She choked back a sob.

"You're courageous." Bella clasped her hands together.

"I know!" *I'm trying to be*. Arm back, Sage thrust the spike forward, into the creature's mouth. It gagged and gurgled. "Die! This is for my teacher."

ChepiTwo jerked, biting the spike, swinging her to the side.

Nate wrapped his arms around her waist, keeping her from falling. Patrick rushed over and held both her shoulders to steady her. She felt the damp blood from his hand.

She regained her balance and shoved harder. Her arm muscles strained to direct the spike, her hands slippery from the moisture of its foul breath and spit. She nearly gagged.

A wail came from the creature. It shriveled and wriggled. Its body swirled beneath the grotesque head. Sage fumbled not to drop the spike, her knuckles white, hands shaking.

Then ChepiTwo whined like a sick cat, and sank into a stinking pile that fast spread out and seeped into the floor.

Sage pulled the spike to her. It was clean, sparkling even. Her breath wheezed out. "Is it gone?"

"It's gone, Miss Emery." Huntley came beside her, his gaze warm. "I wish I could have helped. But you had to do it, alone. Well done, young lady."

Bella clapped her hands, her braids swinging. She looked at Sage, her smile broad, and waved goodbye as she floated up and vanished into the air.

Bella, find peace, Sage called in her mind, her eyes wet with tears. She wondered if Huntley would also dissolve. A deep loss filtered through her, adding to the aches in her body, the reeling of her head.

"Girl, that was sick—awesome." Patrick laughed, eyes wild, his shirt stained with blood. "I can't believe any of this."

"A horrible creature," Nate said, his voice breathy. "But I could have—"

"You could have, I know." Sage hugged him against her. "You saved me. We won."

Legs shaking, her body drained, she wanted to collapse onto the floor.

Chapter 29

Sage read one of the last entries in the diary. *My mother hardly talks to me now. I tried to reach her in a séance, but she wouldn't come. She said she had to wait for the right being to wipe the sins from the manor. Maybe someone not even born yet. Someone who had to be connected by family. A descendant with a special mission. I suppose I won't live to see who it is. Young Jenny enjoys my tarot readings and seances. Could she be the one? But I have doubts. My daughter Jean is mortified at my dealings with the otherworld. I try not to involve her in any of my "practices." She is a shy, unassuming young lady. I'm certain my flamboyance stifled her. The poor thing. I always used it as a distraction, from my transient life.*

An entry weeks later:

Now my mother doesn't speak at all to me. My headaches have faded. I think a child of Jenny's may be the one we're waiting for. But the blood-connect will come through the man she marries.

The August humidity clung to Sage's skin as she walked with Lilah and the boys through the woodsy canopy of trees. The shadowy forest soon made it cooler. Today, she finally felt steady enough to approach the manor.

"The trim I did for the singed parts of your hair looks natural," Lilah said.

"It does. And I'm still covering my burns with makeup. They weren't too bad. Mom *would* be suspicious about what game we were playing." Four days had passed since the ChepiTwo incident, and Sage pretended not to feel well for two of them, to keep her parents at bay. And she needed the rest.

"I don't want all the details, but it must have been dangerous and so high-key." Lilah flipped her long hair behind her shoulder.

"Aunt Jenny did a great job bandaging me up." Patrick showed his arm like a badge of honor. It smelled of antibacterial cream. He winked at Lilah. "I was like a knight in his shiny armor. Come over later for cake to celebrate my fifteenth birthday."

"She's invited. If your arm gets infected, you need to see a doctor." Sage pointed a finger at him. Patrick had refused to go. "You will keep insisting a regular dog and not a coyote attacked you?"

"We both will. Mine weren't deep scratches." Nate shrugged. "Mom was still angry and said to stay out of the forest. She suspects we lied about where we were."

"Uncle Ron is worried about rabies. We don't want those shots." Patrick chuckled.

"If you froth at the mouth, you may have to," Sage said with a tease in her voice.

"I hope we don't meet this animal. You said it was large and not like anything you'd seen before? Sounds extra cursed to me." Lilah glanced around her. Birds twittered, but nothing rustled in the bushes. Their steps crunched over dead leaves and pine needles—releasing a resin scent—from the previous fall.

"It was extra cursed. And the beast huge. You'd be scared. We all were, me for only a minute. But I could protect you." Patrick wriggled his eyebrows. Lilah stuck out her tongue.

"Oh, please. Girls can protect themselves." Sage squared her shoulders. "The animal is gone." At least she hoped it was. Nothing haunted her dreams. She only missed Bella's occasional slip into her sleep. Was the girl really gone, too? Released from the manor and on to paradise. What about Huntley and Miss Dora?

Her stomach dipped. Did she have to say goodbye to all of them? Especially Huntley.

"I don't need protection, except from my noisy family. My dad is retiring from the navy in September. But he'll work as a consultant for a contractor. And order us to keep shipshape." Lilah made a mock salute. "My youngest brother will be hung from the yardarm for his pranks."

Sage laughed, glad she still could after her beast killing. No nightmares—was it more ghost magic? The latex monster she'd created in her room had melted off the head and into a blob. Her family seemed all right now. Nate had taken the bloody incident well, just relieved it was over. Patrick, he'd always be a bragging guy—sort of like his dad. But his anger had faded.

They reached the clearing, the manor on their left. It looked more forlorn than usual, as if an empty shell.

"Has everyone moved out?" Lilah asked. "You had quite the adventure in there. Not that I really want to know."

"I guess they must have moved." Sage remembered something her mom once said. Sometimes people—or ghosts in this case—came into your life for a season, for a reason, then they're gone.

"Will they tear the manor down?" Nate asked.

"I hope not," Sage blurted. Why did a tiny part of the place still tug at her? As if everything inside might wait for her should she desire it.

"I no longer want to explore there. I don't need to be so mental." Patrick shoved his thumbs in the pockets of his jeans. "Soon I'll be home, looking after my mom. Then I start my sophomore year. Football, here I come."

"And we'll be over the causeway at high school. A big change." Lilah smiled. "We need a mall shopping day on the mainland. New clothes to show off."

Sage scanned the house's blank windows. "Yeah, new clothes, to show how grown up we are. How we've matured."

"Aunt Theresa is coming for the birthday party, isn't she?" Nate asked.

"She is." Sage continued to study the manor.

Lilah pressed her shoulder. "Are you okay?"

"Sure, just lots of thoughts." Sage looked at the pond where the ducks skimmed the water. Then at the branch where Mr. Saunders was found. She envisioned her teacher walking around, in one piece, and inspecting the house. Then a child with long red braids frolicking in the high grass. A blonde woman in a long dress plucking wildflowers. Her Grandma Esther on the front porch supervising servants at a lawn party. The odd Miss Dora having tea, laughing with her guests. Did Sage avenge them all?

"I'll miss the spooky stuff, a little," Nate said. "But I'm glad that one thing...is gone. And I was brave. I'm going to the library and check out all their books on forensics. Then I'll ask Dad for a microscope kit."

"You were fearless, my little bro. So was I. We'll find other adventures. Okay, our last look. Let's go back." Patrick turned. "We can try the new pickle ball court in town until my mom comes." He strutted down the path. Nate followed.

"He's changed, hasn't he?" Lilah giggled. "So, your ghosts don't speak to you anymore?"

"It seems that way." Sage wondered if the house was full of dust and cobwebs and the back garden had shriveled up. Would the statue ever find its head?

"You'll forget them. I plan to shine in my audition for Sandy in *Grease*." Lilah sang a high note. "We'll be bigger than this little island."

"You'll be perfect. And I'll dazzle with my makeup skills, to set the 1950s mood. We'll be famous." Sage squeezed her friend's hand. "Go with them. I just need a few minutes."

"If you're sure. Don't be long. You solved the mystery of Mr. Saunders. You should be proud. Though I find it hard to believe." Lilah rubbed Sage's shoulder, then left her.

Sage blew out a slow breath. Solved the mystery, but she could never tell the police or her teacher's family. No one would believe her. They'd haul her off to intense counseling.

Part of growing up was letting go, she decided. But she'd learned compassion and courage from her misadventure here. She glanced up at a second-floor window. She swore she saw movement.

The sash opened. Huntley stood there, half in shadow. He nodded and smiled.

Sage smiled and raised her hand.

Then his body rippled and dissolved into sparks of light, like fireflies. Had she imagined it?

She felt a pinch of sadness, her eyes dampening. Then satisfaction filled her up. She could become a ghost hunter—if her aura remained. Shaking her head, she suspected that was too dangerous. Though a flicker inside convinced her that she and Huntley could meet again someday. She had learned one thing, to forgive. Forgive Grandma Esther, and her father. It helped ease the weight she carried as her life changed. Turning her back on Lakeluster House, she hurried to catch up with the others.

The End

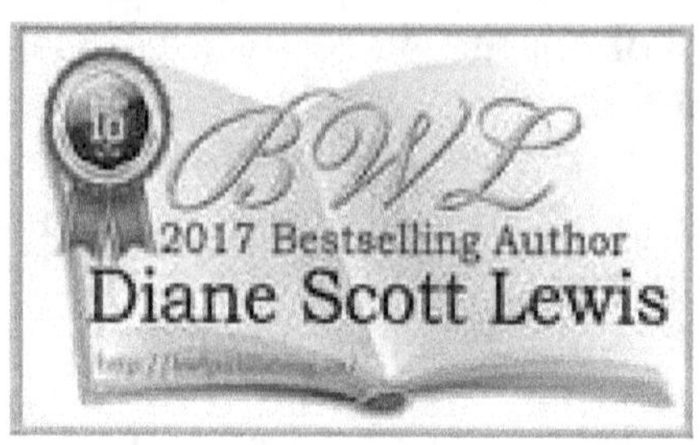

Diane Parkinson (Diane Scott Lewis) has written since age ten and lived all over the world. She wrote book reviews for the *Historical Novel Reviews* magazine and worked as an on-line historical editor from 2007 to 2010. She is a member of the *Historical Novel Society*. Most of her novels are set in late eighteenth-century England, but she's delved into WWII. This is her first young adult novel. She lives in western Pennsylvania with one naughty dachshund. Jorja is the author's granddaughter and an honor student at a western Pennsylvania high school. She has another novel published independently and has won several literary awards.

Diane Scott Lewis books also published by BWL Publishing

Escape the Revolution
Ladies and Their Lovers (Miss Grey's Shady Lover/ The Defiant Lady Pencavel)
Rose's Precarious Quest
The Apothecary's Widow

A Savage Exile – Vampires with Napoleon
on St. Helena
Hostage to the Revolution (continuation of
Escape the Revolution)
On a Stormy Primeval Shore
Her Vanquished Land
Ghost Point
Bretagne-a forbidden affair

For further information about the author,
visit her BWL author page and her blog:
https://www.bookswelove.com/lewis-
diane-scott/
        https://dianescottlewisauthor.blogspot